# Spid

Ursula Moray Williams

Illustrated by David McKee

RED FOX

A Red Fox Book

Published By Random House Children's Books
20 Vauxhall Bridge Road, London SW1V 2SA

A division of The Random House Group Ltd
London Melbourne Sydney Auckland
Johannesburg and agencies throughout the world

First published by Andersen Press, 1985
Beaver Edition 1988
Red Fox edition 1990
This Red Fox edition 2000

Text copyright © Ursula Moray Williams, 1985
Illustrations © Andersen Press Limited, 1985

1 3 5 7 9 10 8 6 4 2

This book is sold subject to the condition that it shall not, by
way of trade or otherwise, be lent, resold, hired out, or otherwise circulated without the publisher's prior consent in any
form of binding or cover other than that in which it is published
and without a similar condition including this condition being
imposed on the subsequent purchaser

The right of Ursula Moray Williams and David McKee to be identified
as the author and illustrator of this work has been asserted by them in
accordance with the Copyright, Designs and Patents Act, 1988

Printed and bound in Denmark by
Nørhaven A/S, Viborg

Papers used by Random House are natural,
recyclable products made from wood grown in sustain-
able forests. The manufacturing processes conform to the
environmental regulations of the country of origin.

THE RANDOM HOUSE GROUP Limited Reg. No. 954009

www.randomhouse.co.uk

ISBN 0 09 940172 X

# CONTENTS

*For Suzanne John*

# 1

## The Arrival of Spid

It was a long, long way up the wastepipe, but by now the spider had climbed most of it, and was still climbing.

First one leg came out of the plughole and then another, and then another and then another and then another and then another and then another and then another.

Spid had arrived.

'I thought spiders only had six legs,' said the boy who was looking over the edge of the bath, 'but I've been counting yours and I thought they would never stop. You are the biggest spider I have ever seen! Are you sure you only have *eight* legs? You haven't left any down there? Where do you come from, anyway?'

The spider explained that he had been trying to get into the house for some weeks, because hiding in a coalshed was not his idea of happiness. He loved people, he said, and he wanted people to love him too.

'*I* love spiders,' said the boy, 'but nobody else does, not in this house! My mother screams when she sees one. My father stamps on them!'

'Ouch!' exclaimed the spider, twitching its feet.

'I know,' the boy agreed, 'but that is why you can't come to live here, I'm afraid. Besides, my grandmother is coming to stay, and she feels faint if she even catches sight of a spider, and our lady helper catches them in dusters and shakes them out of the window.'

'Aiee!' said the spider, bunching itself into a ball.

'My Aunty Bloss traps them in a toothglass and puts them in the boiler,' continued the boy. 'You do see why you can't come and live here, don't you?'

The spider uncurled itself a little and staggered back on to its eight furry legs.

'I've tried all down the road,' it said, 'but they're still worse. But it doesn't matter . . . . ' Slowly and sadly it began the task of getting its eight legs back into the plughole.

First one leg went in, and then another and another . . . .

'Stop!' cried the boy when only two legs were left outside.

The spider looked up hopefully.

'What's your name?' the boy asked.

'Spid.'

'Mine's Henry.'

'Good morning, Henry.'

'Good morning, Spid.'

There was a pause.

'Goodbye, Henry,' said Spid.

'Goodbye, Spid,' said Henry.

There was another pause.

Slowly the spider withdrew two feet. Now he had four legs inside the plughole and four left outside.

A voice from downstairs shouted:

'Haven't you had your bath yet, Henry? Do

hurry up!'

'Nice to have seen you, Spid,' said Henry.

'Yes,' said Spid.

He put three legs into the plughole at once.

'Go on,' said Henry with his hand on the taps, 'I don't want to drown you!'

'I know,' said Spid, ducking into the plughole. He saw the bath plug descending on top of his head, and the light was shut out. The next minute the plug was fast in the hole, but it had caught the end of his last foot, and he dangled inside the pipe unable to move up or down. Also, it hurt.

He waited for the tapwater to batter down upon the top of his head and hoped it would not be too hot. If his leg were free he could have escaped before the water came, but now he would have to wait until the boy had finished his bath, and whichever way it happened, it was sure to be uncomfortable. He made one final effort before the taps were turned on, and called:

'HENRY!'

To the spider's surprise there came a plop! as the plug was pulled out above his head. Daylight arrived, and his eighth leg was free.

Henry's face peered down at him.

'So you're still there!' he exclaimed. 'Aren't you afraid of being drowned? Why didn't you go back the way you came, you silly whatsit? I mean . . . I'm sorry! But you really are rather a stupid sort of spider.'

'You shut my toe in the plug,' Spid said reproachful-

10

ly. 'I would have been miles away by now if only you had been more careful.' He was rapidly climbing away down the wastepipe.

'Oh I *am* sorry! I *am*!' came Henry's voice, and Spid could see his anxious eye looking at him from above. 'Did it pinch you? Did it hurt?'

'Yes,' said Spid, descending rapidly.

'Oh don't go away,' the boy was begging him. 'I didn't mean it. Come back! I'll get you out of the bath before I run it. You can sit in my dressing-gown pocket. Do come back!'

Spid stopped, and very slowly began to climb up the pipe again. He liked the boy's voice, and the boy's face, and the boy's name, and he liked the look of the bathroom and the smell of the soap, and he very much liked the idea of making his new home inside a dressing-gown pocket. It sounded so much more homely than a coal cellar.

He arrived at the top of the wastepipe and put a leg over the edge of the plughole, followed by all the other legs . . . .

Henry stooped over the bath and picked him up, just as a hand banged on the door and a voice shouted:

'Henry! *Will* you get on with your bath? You are going to be late for school!'

'Yes, Dad,' the boy said, hastily turning on the taps. He pushed Spid into his dressing-gown pocket.

'Now you stay there for the present,' he commanded him. 'I've told you all kinds of horrible things may

11

happen to you if people see you running about the house. If our helper, Mrs Gridley, knows I've let you free in the bathroom she won't rest till she's got you, and that's for sure! You may not be so lucky next time you try to come up into the bath—it might be my dad . . . stamp! stamp! Or my mother . . . *aieee—eee*! Or even my Aunty Bloss, and *she'd* catch you in a toothglass and put you down the loo!'

The bathwater was flowing freely now, and Spid peered out gratefully from Henry's pocket as he hung his dressing-gown on a hook behind the door.

'I think you are lovely,' said Henry from the bath. 'All those furry feet! Those shiny round black eyes! Is it the first time you have been in a proper family home, Spid?'

'Not exactly,' said the spider, 'I have visited two or three but I've never got so far as this. I have always been chased out again, or washed down the pipe with the bathwater. It is very kind of you to have me in your house,' he added.

'That's all right,' said Henry, soaping himself. 'I have always needed a spider of my own. But don't make it awkward for me, will you, because my family won't like me to have a spider for a pet. For a friend, I mean . . . ' he corrected himself hastily.

'I know,' the spider said, 'I will be very careful.'

'You had better go on living in my pocket while I am at school,' Henry said, having finished his bath. 'You are as safe there as anywhere really. What do you need to eat?'

'Flies!' said Spid promptly. 'But I've been eating them all night and I shan't need any more till about Friday. Or if I'm hungry in between,' he added, 'I can go back to the coal cellar and get some out of my larder. I've got half a dozen tied up in my web in the cellar window. Big fat ones!'

'Oh Spid! Are they dead?' Henry asked, horrified.

'I should think so!' Spid said cheerfully.

'They are *creatures*,' Henry said to him reproachfully.

'Yummy—yummy!' said Spid, smacking his lips.

'You wouldn't like it if I caught *you* and put you in a cage to eat,' said Henry.

'No I wouldn't,' Spid agreed.

'Well then,' said Henry.

'Yes,' said Spid, waving his feet. 'Yummy—yummy!'

'Hen-*ry*!' came the call from downstairs.

'All *right*!' called Henry. 'I'll bring you breadcrumbs,' he promised the spider as he left the room. 'Forget about the flies. And don't get out of my pocket unless you are absolutely sure there is nobody about. Goodbye, Spid.'

'Goodbye, Henry.' Spid was left alone in Henry's pocket, hanging on the bathroom door.

## 2

### Spid Comes to Stay

The spider stayed quietly in Henry's dressing-gown pocket for two hours after Henry had gone to school.

He heard Henry's father go to work, and Henry's mother stacking up the breakfast plates in the kitchen sink. Then he heard her put on her coat and go out shopping.

'Now I am absolutely certain there is nobody about,' Spid said to himself, and he repeated: 'Now I am absolutely certain . . . .'

He was carefully pulling his legs out of Henry's pocket when he heard the street door open, and somebody marched in quite purposefully, as if they knew the place, and had every right to be there.

'Grandma?' thought Spid, getting back into the pocket. 'Or Aunty Bloss? Henry's mother come back to find her purse?' But it was none of these people. It was Mrs Gridley come to clean the house. She began working in the kitchen, and Spid thought he had time to explore the upper landing, but almost at once she began to come upstairs, clattering her dustpan and brush.

Spid, did he but know it, was in the most terrible danger. He bolted back into the dressing-gown pocket and crouched in the bottom while Mrs Gridley came into Henry's bedroom. She had her own ideas where a boy ought to hang his dressing-gown, and it was not on

14

the back of the bathroom door. She took it off the hook and put it away in Henry's cupboard.

Spid held his breath. Before he was shut up in the cupboard he peeped out of the pocket, and saw a pleasant square room with pictures and posters and calendars covering every inch of the walls. From the ceiling hung mobiles, looking very like himself, only none of the aeroplanes, hawks, butterflies, birds and spacecraft had eight such magnificent legs as he had, nor such shining black eyes. And they hung motionless on their threads where Henry had tied them, quite unable to pull themselves up or let themselves down.

The moment Mrs Gridley had finished rattling round the walls with her dustpan, and roaring round the floor with her vacuum cleaner, which frightened Spid even more than the dustpan, he crawled out of the pocket, squeezed through the keyhole in the cupboard, and dropped down on to the carpet.

But he was not quite quick enough, for Mrs Gridley had not yet closed the door, and now she was back again to fetch her duster.

'You great black monster!' she cried, pounding across the carpet. 'How could I miss you? Just you wait, my hairy friend! I'll soon have you back where you belong.'

Spid rushed underneath the bed.

Mrs Gridley lay across the top of the bed and swatted at him as he appeared the other side. The corner of the duster flashed so close beside his head that he was knocked off balance, and lay kicking with all eight legs in the air.

As Mrs Gridley jumped off the bed to pick him up, Spid found his balance and fled into the darkest corner he could see. He dared not leave the shadows while she was hovering over the bed with her duster, so he curled himself into a tight black ball, closed his eyes, and waited.

Presently he opened them for a peep, and saw Mrs Gridley's head hanging upside down over the edge of Henry's bed, her eyes moving from corner to corner in search of him. He could feel her moving down the bed, closer and closer to the corner where he lay, and very carefully he uncoiled and began to climb up the wall behind the bedleg.

While Mrs Gridley still peered and searched and made feeble little sallies with her duster, Spid dashed over the pillow, fled across the sheet, scrambled over her prostrate form, traversed a chair and a box and a pile of books, and was up the opposite curtain hanging by a thread from the ceiling while she was on her hands and knees below, still looking for him under the bed.

Spid hung there among the cardboard mobiles, enjoying himself, and quite out of Mrs Gridley's reach. He giggled as she squeezed herself flat underneath the bed, and backed out again the same way, after which she flapped the duster under the chest of drawers and all the other furniture.

Finally she stood upright, very hot and puzzled, and

16

almost immediately caught sight of him hanging among the mobiles from the ceiling.

'Ah—you little reptile, you!' she shouted, and this time her flapping duster caught two mobile paper pheasants and a space ship, and brought them crashing to the ground. Spid escaped by leaping on to the cable of the electric light, and while Mrs Gridley was sorrowfully gathering up the fragments of Henry's treasures he let himself down soberly to the floor, and left the room.

The street door opened again, and this time it was Henry's mother back from the shops.

Mrs Gridley appeared at the bedroom door.

'There has been a most terrible big spider in Henry's bedroom,' she announced. 'The biggest I ever saw in my life! Eight legs if it had one!'

'They all have eight legs, Mrs Gridley,' said Henry's mother, looking pale, but smiling.

'I tried to chase it out,' Mrs Gridley said, 'but I'm afraid while I was doing it Henry's mobiles got in the way.' She held out the pieces. 'The spider was hanging from the ceiling, the great brute!' she explained. 'And my duster caught up in Henry's bits and pieces. I always thought they asked for it,' she added, looking aggrieved. 'I tell my Norman he can only have two hanging up at a time . . . but he says Henry has as many as he wants, so what can I say to him? But I never saw a spider that size in *my* house,' said Mrs Gridley stoutly.

'Oh how dreadful! Did you get it out?' Henry's

mother cried.

'No I didn't! But I will before I'm done,' Mrs Gridley promised.

She went back into Henry's room and banged about again with the dustpan, and finally with the hoover. She moved first the bed and then all the furniture, and shook out all the pillows.

Henry's mother pretended she had letters to write, and sat at her desk with her feet tucked high up above the floor.

Spid was too considerate to venture near her. He went into the kitchen, keeping an ear open for Mrs Gridley's footsteps, or Henry's mother, or the electricity man, or anybody else likely to be paying calls in the middle of the morning.

The more he saw of it the more convinced he became that this was the house he would like to live in. He felt sure he could cope with the people in it; it was only a question of time. Best to stay out of the way as much as possible at first, especially while Henry was at school. And best always to wipe his feet, all eight of them, and not to leave cobwebs around. And best of all, to do all his exploring at night, round the edges of the room rather than across the middle, especially by daylight.

'I wonder where I had better keep my flies,' thought Spid, making future plans. In the end he decided to keep them in the bathroom, under the bath, where it was handy for fetching them up the wastepipe.

Henry came home from school. He raced up to the

bathroom, found his dressing-gown gone, and went roaring to his mother.

'Where's my dressing-gown gone?'

'Where it belongs, I should imagine,' said his mother. 'Have you looked in your cupboard?'

Henry found his dressing-gown in his cupboard, with Spid asleep inside the pocket, and nearly hugged him with joy. 'It was an awful day,' Henry told him. 'I didn't like anybody at school, it was one of those days. I was only thinking about you.'

'I didn't like anybody either,' said Spid, spinning loving threads round Henry's buttons. 'They were all terrible to me while you were gone! I nearly got destroyed between the lot of them. But I never thought about thinking about you.'

'I was afraid you might have gone back to your coal cellar,' Henry said, 'and I had no idea how I would find you if you had.'

'That's right,' Spid agreed. 'But I didn't think of that either.'

'I'm glad you didn't,' Henry said. 'Do you think you are going to enjoy living in this house?'

'Oh yes,' said Spid. 'But as you see, I shall have to be very careful at first. I have so many enemies. I am much cleverer, but they are stronger than me.'

'I shan't let them kill you,' Henry said stoutly. 'But I can't protect you if you insist on running into danger. I've told you that before. Please, please take care, and don't do anything stupid!'

'I can run fast,' Spid boasted.

'So can my dad,' said Henry. 'And it's no good having eight legs if they all get stepped on at the same moment. I can't save you if I'm not there to do it, can I? And if my mother tells my dad to kill you . . . he *will!*'

'All right, Henry,' promised Spid.

# 3

## Spid the Rescuer

In bed that night Henry confessed to his mother that he had a special spider for a pet.

'Oh *no*, Henry! Not a spider!' said his mother, quite appalled.

'It's a splendid spider, Mum. Not an ordinary one,' Henry insisted. 'Eight furry legs—so strong and clean and hairy! Shiny black eyes! It's *good!* It eats flies in the coal cellar.'

Henry's mother detested flies even more than she detested spiders. There were so many more of them, and they buzzed.

'Oh Henry,' she said helplessly.

'I want my spider *saved*,' Henry said, seizing the opportunity. 'I want it taken care of, and not stamped on or swatted at or put down the loo. I want to feel certain it is safe in the house while I am at school. Mrs Gridley mustn't shake it out of the window, and if Aunty Bloss comes to the house she's not to put it in the boiler.'

'Oh well, Henry,' said his mother meekly.

'Or else . . . we'll always have flies in the house!' Henry finished up threateningly.

'All right, Henry.'

'Promise?'

'Yes, I promise, Henry,' said his mother, but she felt rather unhappy, and went down to talk to his father

22

about it.

'Don't worry! He'll soon get tired of it, like the silkworms,' his father said.

But it made Henry's mother very nervous. On the days that Mrs Gridley did not work in the house she crept about opening doors and saying, 'Shoo!' before she went into any of the rooms.

Spid was usually behind, and not in front of her. He thought it was kinder, and he simply could not stay all day long shut up in Henry's dressing-gown pocket. He liked Henry's mother very much, and hoped that one day they might make friends, but it did not seem very likely at present.

Then one day he found her crying in the bathroom. She had been wiping down the bath and her wedding ring had slipped off her finger and vanished down the plughole. She fished for it with a nail file, a bobby pin and a piece of picture wire. All in vain. The ring was gone.

Spid walked boldly across the bathroom floor and up the side of the bath.

Henry's mother saw him, but she was too upset to scream. She just went on crying, while the spider let himself down into the bath and disappeared into the wastepipe after the ring.

If she was relieved to see him disappear Henry's mother showed no sign of it, and she did not put the plug back in the bath. Neither did she stop crying for a moment, but gave a feeble little moan of disgust as one by one the spider's legs reappeared over the edge of the plughole, and Spid climbed out.

He was not carrying the wedding ring, but he attached himself to the top of the cold tap and began to pull in after himself a long silken thread that reached down the wastepipe . . . down, down, down and out of sight.

Then he began to draw it in.

Henry's mother watched him. She wished he would go away so she could go on fishing for her ring, perhaps with a little magnet. Only magnets do not pick up gold or silver, and by now the ring might be travelling down the drain, further and further away towards the sea.

Spid went on drawing in his thread, and presently, against the side of the pipe below could be heard a faint tinkle.

Henry's mother stopped crying and sat up suddenly. She leaned forward and peeped through her fingers.

Spid was still winding in his thread, which gleamed like dull gold in the light from the window. The tinkling grew louder.

Then, with a little rattle, something bounced out of the dark plughole into the bath.

It was Henry's mother's wedding ring, tied to the end of a long spider's thread that Spid was even now tucking under one of his eight arms or wherever else he kept it. Henry's mother could hardly believe her eyes.

'You simply wonderful, *clever* little spider!' she told him gratefully, picking up the ring.

Spid knew better than to answer her. Besides, there was nothing more to be said. He sat quite quietly on the bath tap until she had left the room, and then he wove such a strong mesh across the plughole that nothing could be lost down it again. Spid now had two of the family on his side.

He heard Henry's mother telling Mrs Gridley about it in the morning. She had already told Henry and Henry's father.

'It *deliberately* went down the wastepipe and fished up my ring,' she repeated. 'I couldn't have believed it if I hadn't seen it with my own eyes!'

Henry's father laughed.

'Well, if it has cured you of your phobia about spiders, hip-hip-hooray!' he said. 'Just let me know if I'm treading on a good one or a bad one! They all look alike to me!'

'I don't want you to tread on *any* of them,' said Henry's mother firmly. 'I feel much too grateful. Besides, I promised Henry that you shouldn't. It isn't kind.'

'That isn't what you said last week,' said Henry's father, but Spid kept a wary eye on him and stayed out of his way.

The next person to make friends with was Mrs Gridley, who had not really believed Henry's mother's story, but when she found Spid polishing the kitchen window panes her feeling for spiders changed. Mrs Gridley was very proud of her windows. Silently she

25

tore rags into eight little dusters and put them into Spid's eight hands.

'Thank you, ma'am,' said Spid.

'I never would have believed it,' Mrs Gridley said aloud, watching him. 'You would think it had been brought up to it, the way it works! There's only one thing that worries me,' she added, seeing Spid busy on the outside of the glass. 'If one of them birds in the garden, or a great, fat pussycat made up its mind to pick you off, who's going to stop it?'

Spid stopped short and gave a terrified glance in all directions, but there was no bird and no pussycat to be seen. It was a thought, however.

'It seems to me,' Mrs Gridley mused, 'that while you are polishing on the outside I should be doing it on the inside and that way nobody is going to dare to come and hurt you, you poor little beast!'

Spid welcomed the idea of working in company with Mrs Gridley, who did not really want to give up all her lovely windows, so they were both quite content. When she was absent Spid stayed inside the glass, and when the birds made dabs at the panes, or a large fat pussycat landed on the sill outside he realised that there was a great deal of sense in Mrs Gridley's warning.

They enjoyed working in partnership, and Spid had made another friend in the family.

# 4

## Spid and Grandpa

Grandpa Pratt came to stay once or twice a year, usually in the summer. He was a pink and white old gentleman, his face surrounded by fluffy whiskers. He had very blue eyes and a mouth which he used very little, except for grumbling and eating.

Nobody ever heard him say thank you, yet no one could call him ungrateful, for he had a little flip of his fingers and a nod of his head that said it for him. Mrs Gridley called him a dear old gentleman.

Before he arrived the house was turned upside down making a bedroom for him downstairs. Henry thought this was better than turning out of his own bedroom, as he did for Grandma, his mother's mum, who refused to sleep on the ground floor. She said people could look at her through the window, and she never had any faith in lace curtains.

Fortunately the two of them never came to stay at the same time, and these were the only grandparents Henry had. He warned Spid that spiders were likely to be unpopular with both his relations.

'But I only want to be friends,' grumbled Spid.

'Well, just be friends all by yourself in a corner,' Henry advised him, 'because Grandpa may look old and helpless but he has got ever such a long reach with a newspaper. He smashed up my model aircraft when it flew round his head, and you would never have

27

thought he could get near it.'

Spid went and sulked in Henry's room. He felt jealous when he heard Henry's mother making a fuss of the old gentleman.

'We've put you downstairs, Grandpa,' she told him when he arrived. 'We knew you would find the stairs trying, with your legs!'

'There's nothing wrong with my legs,' Grandpa retorted. 'It's my knees that are stiff, that's all! And I can easily sleep upstairs. You can put the boy downstairs. He'll be out of my way . . . .'

'Oh Grandpa! And last time you made us change it all when you went to bed!' protested Mrs Pratt, at her wits' end.

'That was last time!' snapped Grandpa. 'Besides, the spiders came in from the garden, and I hardly got any sleep at all.'

'There,' Henry muttered to Spid. 'You heard what he said! Now, you keep right out of his sight—do you hear?'

'I only wanted to be friends,' grumbled Spid.

But before they could change all the arrangements again Grandpa decided that he did not want to sleep upstairs after all; to everybody's great relief he settled down in the lower room and closed all the windows.

Henry did not see very much of his grandfather, who got up at about half past ten in the morning and retired soon after seven at night, drinking hot drinks at eleven, coffee at two, tea at four, with nice little meals on trays

28

at one o'clock. He had his evening meal in bed.

As a grandfather he was a failure, Henry thought, but at least it was something that Mrs Gridley's Norman could not be jealous about, even though he had no grandpa of his own.

The boys spent much of their free time together, and on Saturday morning, when they had gone off to fish, Spid left the shelter of the house to take a turn in the garden by himself since it was a pleasantly fine and sunny day.

He ambled and rambled round the borders, making little darts sideway to make the ants and ladybirds jump, or dodging any hungry-looking blackbirds and thrushes that stopped their singing for a brief moment in search of some refreshment. In between times he basked in the sunshine underneath a warm stone, or idly spun a web round and round a sunflower stem, before making a still wider loop round the trunk of a cherry tree.

While he was spinning this latest loop the door of the house opened, and out came Mrs Pratt, carrying a folding chair, followed by Grandpa carrying his stick, and between them quite a number of useful articles such as a newspaper, a footstool and a cup of coffee.

Mrs Pratt placed the chair underneath the cherry tree. Grandpa sat in it, decided he wanted to face the other side of the garden, and got up again with groans and great difficulty and some tugging and pulling by Mrs Pratt.

'It's not my legs,' Grandpa complained, kicking his stick and the newspaper in all directions. 'It's my knees that are stiff; there's nothing wrong with the rest of me at all!'

'I know, I know, Grandpa,' Mrs Pratt soothed him. 'Mrs Brown and Mr Duke and Major Tuckett and the Bishop all say the same . . . .'

'No they don't!' roared Grandpa. 'They've all got leg trouble. All the lot of them! I've seen 'em! There's nothing wrong with *my* legs. It's just my knees.'

'Yes Grandpa,' said Mrs Pratt, putting his coffee cup into his hands.

Spid shot up the tree into the branches above and sat looking down on Grandpa, who waited only for Henry's mother to reach the house before calling her back again to pick up his paper.

It was a pity, Spid thought, that the old gentleman could not do these things for himself. All he needed, after all, was something like a rope to hang on to and give him his balance, and then he would not have to worry other people to wait on him. Especially if it were true that only his knees prevented him from getting around without help.

And if it were only the question of a rope . . . ?

Very carefully Spid began to unwind a length of strong, silken thread above Grandpa's head. It was his very best quality of web, and it descended inch by inch on to Grandpa, shining in the morning sun.

At the same time a large, fat bluebottle came droning

30

across the garden and became interested in the old man sitting in his dressing-gown underneath the cherry tree, with his coffee cup in his hand. The note in its buzzing altered. It lost interest in the cherry blossom and began to make noisy circles round Grandpa's saucer.

Grandpa and Spid caught sight of it at the same moment.

Spid made a lunge towards it, and Grandpa swiped. His swipe missed the bluebottle but cut right through Spid's beautiful new thread, from the end of which Spid dropped with a plop! into his coffee cup.

There came a roar like a wounded elephant that echoed round the garden, as Grandpa yelled:

'Help! Mary! Mrs Gridley! Mrs Gridley! Mary! Some of you come out here *now*! There's a spider in my coffee cup!'

Before help came Grandpa had flung the contents of the cup into the nearest flowerbed. Spid had extricated himself, and was running with all eight legs to dry himself on a brick beside the path.

Seeing its chance, a thrush pounced down, and he only escaped sudden death in the nick of time. The thrush tapped its beak on the brick and flew away.

All in all Spid felt safer up the tree.

Panting with nervous exhaustion he ran across the grass to the back of the cherry tree and scuttled up the trunk, just as Mrs Pratt and Mrs Gridley arrived in answer to Grandpa's cries. New coffee was brought,

Grandpa's chair was turned round, he was helped to his feet and helped to sit down again.

'It's my knees,' Grandpa grumbled. 'What I need is a rope to pull on.'

'There,' thought Spid scornfully. 'I could have told him that before.'

This time he waited until the coffee was drunk, and the saucer put down on the grass. The bluebottle stayed away and Grandpa slept.

Spid wove a still more splendid rope, and was careful to keep it coiled on top of the branch until it was long enough to test.

When he uncoiled it and let it down he dangled on the end of it just within reach of Grandpa's hand, and by wrapping up his legs and arms and making himself into a tight, round ball, Spid looked like nothing so much as the bobble on the end of a bell pull.

Then he went to sleep like Grandpa, gently swaying to and fro in the warm summer air.

When he woke the old gentleman was just stirring. Grandpa looked round the garden from underneath his fluffy white eyebrows, and spread his whiskers in an enormous yawn.

He thought it must be time to go in for dinner, and began impatiently to tap his stick on the ground and to look for Henry's mother or Mrs Gridley to come and help him out of his chair.

But it was not so late as Grandpa thought, and Mrs Pratt and Mrs Gridley were busy on the other side of the house. They were not even thinking about Grandpa, and he suspected it. He began to kick his heels in the grass.

After five minutes, when still nobody came, he began to shout, but not very loudly, because he was afraid of bringing out the lady next door, who liked nothing better than to put her head over the wall and have a chat. She even called him Grandpa.

Sure enough, her head appeared, just when he did not want in the least to see her.

'Aren't they coming then?' she asked sympathetically. 'Can't you get up, Grandpa? Shall I come and help you?'

'No,' roared Grandpa, 'I can get up by myself! I don't want any help! There's nothing wrong with my legs! . . . I . . . .'

'I'll telephone them,' the neighbour said soothingly, and disappeared.

Grandpa made a tremendous effort to get out of his chair. One arm flailed about, and caught hold of Spid's rope. He snatched at it, lost it, and snatched again, pulled . . . found it, and hauled himself triumphantly on to his feet.

'There,' said Spid kindly, 'I knew you could if you tried!'

'And what's *your* name?' Grandpa demanded, looking at the rope and at Spid crouching on the end of it.

'Spid, Grandpa sir. My name is Spid.'

'Well, you're a bright fellow,' Grandpa announced, admiringly. 'I never knew a spider as bright as you before. You hang around, see? I can do with a chap like you among all these dunderheads!'

'Yes, Grandpa sir,' said Spid dutifully.

Grandpa stumped towards the house while Spid wound up his thread into the branches of the cherry tree and waited.

In the afternoon Grandpa came out again.

He settled down quite cheerfully in his seat under the cherry tree, and looked around for Spid.

'Spid! Spiddy! Where's that spider? Where the devil are you, Spid?'

'I'm here, Grandpa sir,' said Spid, looking down on Grandpa from the branch where he had been resting.

'That's right then. You stay there till you are wanted,' ordered Grandpa, settling himself in the sun with the newspaper in his hands. It soon fell forward over his eyes and he went to sleep.

'Don't you move, spider,' Grandpa said, just before he dropped off. 'I shall need you presently to help me to get on to my feet.'

'Yes, Grandpa sir,' Spid replied smartly.

'S'not my legs ... s'my ... knees ... ' Grandpa muttered with his face falling into the pages of the newspaper. 'S'nothing wrong ... with ... my ... legs ... .'

Spid had already gone back to sleep. He was well on

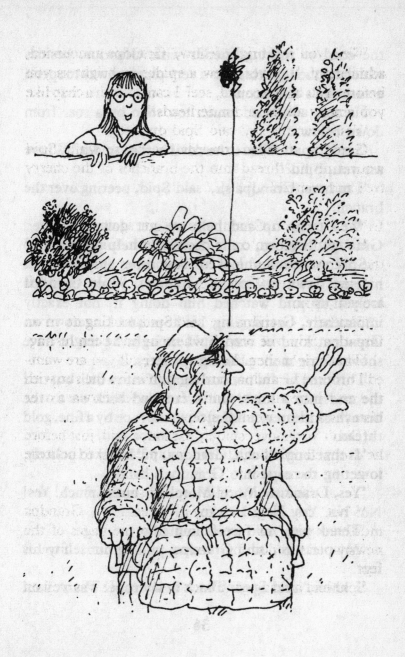

the road to making friends with Grandpa, besides which he thought this was a very pleasant way to spend a summer's afternoon.

He was awakened much too soon by a roar from down below.

'Spid! Spid! Where the devil is that spider? Where are you, Spid?'

'I'm here, Grandpa sir,' said Spid, peering over the branch.

'Well come up and help me get down,' ordered Grandpa. 'I mean, come down and help me get up!'

Spid unwound one of his best ropes and slowly let himself down on top of Grandpa, while Grandpa looked up and watched him doing it, not exactly impatiently, but jiggling his toes and fingers in an impatient kind of way. Spid thought he might have shown some more pleasing manners.

This time he did not curl himself into a ball, but tied the end into a knot, and scrambled back on to the branch of the tree, holding on to the rope by a fine, gold thread.

'Is that long enough, Grandpa sir?' he asked politely, lowering the rope into Grandpa's hand.

'Yes, I think so. More! More! No, not so much! Yes! No! No. Yes. Now I've got it!'

'Thank you,' said Spid pointedly.

'My pleasure,' said Grandpa, pulling himself to his feet.

'I know,' said Spid. 'But it is my rope. Thank you!

Thank you!' At each thank you he gave the rope a little jerk. When this had no effect he twitched it out of Grandpa's hands, and the old gentleman sat down again very suddenly in his chair.

'Why, you double-crossing, crafty, little devil!' roared Grandpa just as Henry came through the gate on his return from fishing.

'What's the matter, Grandpa?' he called, seeing his grandfather's kicking feet. 'Do you want to get up? I'll help you!'

'I don't want your help! I can manage perfectly well by myself!' shouted Grandpa. 'It's that perishing spider up there in the tree. One minute he's getting me up, and then the next he's letting me down. Just wait till I get hold of him!'

Henry saw Spid crouching on the cherry tree branch like an eight-legged miniature jaguar. He saw the malice in Spid's shiny black eyes, and the coils of the beautiful rope he had been weaving.

'Oh Spiddy!' he reproached him. 'What have you been doing to Grandpa?'

In answer, Spid quietly lowered the rope, which arrived in Grandpa's hand. The old gentleman snatched at it and held it so tightly that the branch above quivered.

'There you see,' Grandpa announced. 'Who said I couldn't get myself out of my chair?' He stood there in triumph, facing Henry.

'I think you are wonderfully clever, Grandpa,'

said Henry.

'That's right! So I am!' said Grandpa, beaming.

'And so is Spid,' said Henry.

'Thank you,' said Spid, but he was speaking to Grandpa, not to Henry.

'There you are. Now you know,' said Grandpa, preparing to pick up his walking stick.

Spid slackened the rope, and immediately Grandpa fell back into his chair on top of the newspaper.

'You wait till I get hold of you, you impudent, doublecrossing, little devil!' Grandpa raged, snatching at the silken rope which Spid was twitching and dancing a few inches above his head.

'He only wants you to say "thank you", Grandpa,' Henry reproached him, as the rope was rapidly wound upwards, to disappear among the branches.

'What? Where? Why? Wotchermean?' said Grandpa, quite flabbergasted. The rope came down again and tickled his eyebrows. Grandpa grabbed at it unsuccessfully.

'*Spid!*' pleaded Henry, and at last the spider stopped tormenting, and lowered the rope fairly and squarely into Grandpa's hands. Grandpa hauled on it and pulled himself to his feet.

'Thanks,' he said sheepishly, aiming his word at the branches, but Spid was on the end of the rope. He lowered himself to the ground, put a thread round the end of Grandpa's stick, and twitched it into his hand.

'My pleasure, Grandpa sir,' he said politely.

38

Henry felt rather sore that Grandpa now regarded Spid as his very own and private property.

First thing in the morning while Henry was having his breakfast the cry would go forth from Grandpa's bedroom:

'*Spid! Spid!* Where the devil is that spider?' And Spid would obediently leave Henry's pocket and trot off to Grandpa's room, to be welcomed with cries of: 'So there you are, my little beauty! And how may *you* be this morning?'

Grandpa's manners became much more pleasant in Spid's company. He even called Henry's mother 'my dear'.

'But he shouldn't call Spid *his* spider,' Henry complained bitterly. 'He's *my* spider, and he knows it. Spid knows it, I mean, and Grandpa does too! They're just playing each other up! The next thing is he'll be taking Spid home with him when he leaves here. Just you wait and see!'

'Oh I'm sure he won't, dear,' his mother said soothingly. 'And just think how much more we are enjoying Grandpa's visit because of Spid. He's such a *good* little spider! He never gets in my way in the house, and if I lose a needle or drop a pin he's after it in a minute. He's a dear little spider!'

Mrs Gridley agreed. Spid polished her windows, and kept his fly traps down behind the bath where they got in nobody's way. He never allowed the sight of a cobweb to offend the family, although his webs were

39

his pride and joy, and he knew he spun them better than any other spider in the world. But he would not allow any other spider to come into the house.

Nearly everybody in Henry's home was his friend now.

## 5

## Sick Unto Death

For all his efforts to be helpful and agreeable Spid found it almost impossible to make friends with Henry's father.

Mr Pratt was not afraid of spiders. He just thought they were completely, wholly and utterly unnecessary to a civilised society, and did his best to exterminate them whenever one crossed his path.

Henry had not exaggerated when he told Spid that his father would stamp on him at the earliest opportunity. Mr Pratt would, and nearly did. On more than one occasion Spid had to run for his life, and only escaped by a mere hair's breadth.

'Don't be so ruthless, dear,' Henry's mother pleaded. 'One of these spiders is Henry's pet, and he is such a dear, helpful little fellow!'

'Ha!' said Henry's father. 'Why can't he have a hamster for a pet? Or a rabbit? Or gerbils, like other boys do? If I had tried to make a pet of a spider when I was a boy . . . .'

'He is ever so useful to Grandpa too,' Mrs Pratt said hastily. 'He helps him up and down from his chair and . . . .'

'Grandpa always tells me he doesn't need helping!' Mr Pratt snapped. 'And I'm surprised at you, my dear Mary, for tolerating dirty insects like that around the house. All those legs! Why, Henry brings in enough dirt on two! Mrs Gridley will be leaving us next.'

'She likes Henry's spider,' said Mrs Pratt. 'And the spider helps her to do her work.'

'*Helps her to do her work!*' Mr Pratt repeated, and burst out laughing. 'Well that *is* a good one, I must say!'

Spid quivered with indignation in the mousehole to which he had retired. But he knew it was useless to be angry with Henry's father. He must be persuaded, like Henry's mother and like Mrs Gridley, that some spiders were clever, noble and useful creatures, and all the better for having eight legs instead of two. It was all the more legs to be useful with.

He set about being useful to Henry's father. When a storm of wind wrenched the runner bean sticks away from the wall, Spid climbed up with the utmost care and diligence and secured them so that they would not blow down again.

But Henry's father did not notice the webs that bound them to the wall nails. He thought he had just been lucky in losing no bean rows when most of his neighbours' plants were dashed to the ground.

It quite escaped his notice that Spid had killed the flies on the cabbages, frightened away the white butterflies that laid their eggs in the brussels sprout plants, and made many a weary journey to the fence and back carrying greedy, fat caterpillars, and dropping them through a knot hole to the other side.

It took up all his time while Henry was at school.

Grandpa Pratt had gone home again.

Once Spid was pounced on by a robin, and shaken nearly to death. It took all the strength of his eight powerful feet to kick himself free, and even then the robin hunted him up and down the bean rows, till a wandering cat threatened him in his turn, and he flew away.

The cat looked scornfully at Spid, dabbed at him with a shrouded paw, and strolled out of the garden. Spid waited till it went to sleep on top of a wall, and then spun so many webs around it that the cat took the whole afternoon and half a dozen washings to get its fur free of them again.

'It is Spid that keeps your vegetables so clear from flies,' Henry pointed out to his father when they strolled round the garden on a Sunday morning.

'Really?' said his father disbelievingly. 'That's what you think! One fat, filthy spider? You must be joking!'

Spid was so indignant that he stayed away from the kitchen garden for nearly a week, and the flies and caterpillars all came back again. Mr Pratt sprayed the place with insecticide, just when Spid had made up his mind that he could not bear to see such an infestation. He spent a whole night catching the flies and eating them, and by the morning he had swallowed so much insecticide that he was feeling very ill.

By the time Henry came back from school Spid was very nearly dead.

'Oh Spiddy, what's *wrong* with you?' Henry cried,

when he found the pale, shrivelled and suffering body of his little friend huddled up beside his pillow.

'Bellyache,' murmured Spid, and he turned a shade paler still. 'It's awful. The stuff came off the sprouts . . . .'

Henry did not hesitate. He wrapped Spid tenderly in a handkerchief and bicycled off with him to the vet.

It was late in the day and the surgery was empty. Henry was able to walk straight in and lay the spider's body on the table of the veterinary surgeon, Mr Pawsey.

'And what have we here?' said the vet, looking with some surprise at the suffering spider. 'There's nothing wrong with *that* thing, is there? I should think he's a pretty large fellow when he's stretched out?'

Spid put forward one quivering leg, and then another, finally followed by six more. Each leg was shivering and cold, and looked ready to drop off the pale and shivering body in the middle. The shiny round eyes were nearly closed.

'I *see*,' said the vet, looking concerned. 'It is in a bad way, isn't it? And what do you suppose has happened to it?'

'Bellyache,' said Henry anxiously. 'It has been eating the flies in my dad's vegetable garden, and Dad has been spraying with insecticide, so the insects would have died anyway, only Spid didn't know that, you see. He only wanted to be helpful . . . .'

'Bad luck!' said the vet. He told Spid to put out

44

his tongue.

The tongue that Spid was at last persuaded to put out was only a shadow of the bright pink, lively little flag he usually displayed. He took it back again very quickly and tightly shut his eyes . . . for the last time, thought Henry, in an agony of despair.

'Can't you do *anything* for him?' he asked the vet beseechingly.

'Well—I *could* give him something,' Mr Pawsey admitted thoughtfully, 'but it is a question of persuading him to take it. It tastes very disagreeable, and it might make him sick . . . .'

'Do you hear that, Spid?' Henry said firmly, spreading out his handkerchief and placing the spider in the middle of it. 'It's up to you, Spiddy! Do you want to die . . . or . . . ?'

For an answer, Spid opened both his glazing eyes, even as his eight legs sagged and crumpled underneath his body. A small, pale mouth came open, first hesitatingly and then wider and wider—the tongue was almost white by now.

Henry felt sure he was dying, but Mr Pawsey did not wait long enough to take any chances. He snatched a bottle off a shelf, measured four drops into a salt spoon, and tipped them down the tiny, gaping throat.

Spid gave a tremendous gulp . . . then slithered rather than ran down the table leg, shuffled across the floor into the darkest corner of the room, and disappeared.

'He's gone!' gulped Henry, nearly in tears.

'No, no! Give him a chance!' said Mr Pawsey. 'We got the stuff into him, and he's a brave little chap. Just wait a moment and see what happens.'

Henry waited, and every minute seemed an hour long.

At last, just as he was about to drop on hands and knees and scour every inch of the wainscot for that beloved little dead body, there came a movement in a far corner.

First one leg could be seen marching, and then several more. *Marching*, too, not dragging themselves painfully across the floor as they had done before. There was an unmistakable swagger in Spid's return, each leg was raised and put down as if it wore military trousers, while the body in the middle was radiating health and vigour. The round eyes were shinier than ever, and the pink tongue flashing in and out seemed to be licking its chops as if it were well satisfied with what it tasted.

Spid ignored Henry and ran straight up Mr Pawsey's leg.

'Thank you, Doctor,' he said, perching on his knee. 'You are a very clever vet. I feel quite myself again now. And what do I owe you for the visit?'

Mr Pawsey looked extremely surprised, but also delighted by the success of his treatment.

'Why really . . . ' he began, 'I don't think we'll make any charge for that. It was so . . . well, I mean, if you feel cured that's all the payment I need. I don't think I have ever treated a spider before.'

'Thank you, Doctor! You are a real gentleman, sir!' said Spid, running across the table to find Henry's pocket. 'But if you ever need any help in your surgery, sir . . .any bandaging of wounds, or splinting of broken limbs . . . don't hesitate to call on me! I shall be delighted to be of assistance.'

'Thank *you*,' said Mr Pawsey gratefully.

Henry could only stammer his own thanks. He was quite speechless until they were outside on the pavement again, when he gave Spid a piece of his mind about eating things that had insecticide on them.

'I know! I know!' said Spid impatiently. 'But who was to know that your father was going to do a silly thing like that? He had much better have left the job to *me*!'

# 6
## Cobweb Morning

One beautiful June morning Spid awoke to find dew all over the lawn outside. And in the dew, from one end of the lawn to the other, were spread hundreds and hundreds of miniature spiders' webs, silver with dew-drops, delicate as lace, shining in the morning sun.

Spid was horrified. It was Mrs Gridley's morning to come to work, and he guessed immediately that she would blame the cobwebs at his door. Squeezing underneath the front door he ran rapidly round the outside of the house to see whether the webs were decorating the windows and the window-sills as they were the garden, but there were very few to be seen on the walls of the house, so he ran into the greenhouse and fetched the dolls' house dustpan and brush that was used to clean the smaller pots. With this, and using the greatest care and diligence, he began to sweep the lawn.

Henry's mother saw him at it as she drew the bedroom curtains. 'Oh *no!*' she exclaimed in distress. 'He mustn't! He *mustn't*! It's a cobweb morning, and Henry's spider is sweeping them all away!'

Henry was roused from his bed and sent out to prevent him. It was almost impossible to explain to Spid that what he was doing was wrong. If one cobweb was out of place in the sitting-room, then how could a thousand webs possibly be tolerated on the lawn?

His feelings were so hurt by the family's protests that he decided to go and live with Grandpa.

Grandpa thought it was the greatest joke in the world. He slapped his thighs and told anyone who came near him that he had never met such a spider in his life.

'Tried to clean up the whole garden!' Grandpa laughed, rolling about in his chair. 'And some people can't even dust a bedroom!'

Spid felt he was being laughed at, and ran home to hide in the bathroom wastepipe.

Mrs Pratt saw him disappearing, and very gently but firmly put the plug in the bath. Spid lurked underneath it until he heard Henry and his mother laughing about it together, and then he slid down the wastepipe in a rage and went to sulk in the coal cellar.

# 7
# The Band

'I'm not going back there . . . not ever!' said Spid angrily, turning his back on the coal cellar, the garden and the house.

He marched out of the gate and down the road. For a moment his heart was sore for Henry, till he remembered that Henry had been cool with him lately because of Grandpa's claims . . . and then to go and laugh at him this morning for working so hard and trying to be helpful!

Only Mrs Gridley really understood him, Spid thought. He ambled down the road till he met her coming out of her garden gate pushing her bicycle. When she had gone by without noticing him he slipped into the bicycle shed through a crack in the door.

There were no cobwebs in Mrs Gridley's garden, nor in her shed, nor on the windows of her spotlessly clean little house.

True, she had no real garden to speak of, just a patio, and it had evidently been swept clean before she left for work. The bicycle shed was far too clean and tidy to have spiders' webs in it, and there were no bicycles either, because Mrs Gridley was out, and her boy Norman and her girl Linda were both at school. But although the place looked bare and inhospitable by his standards, it still had a feeling of Mrs Gridley about it, and Spid did not want to crawl back to his own place as if nothing had happened. They didn't deserve to have a spider like him, he thought. So he decided to wait until Mrs Gridley came back from work, and after spinning himself a cosy web in a corner where he thought he would not be noticed, he curled up into a ball and went to sleep.

He awoke quite late in the afternoon.

Outside the light had taken on an afternoon tint. The air was quiet, and smelled a little of bonfires and teatime. And Norman Gridley was just pushing his bicycle into the shed.

Spid looked at him warily. A big boy, bigger than Henry, but rather podgy. His face was pink and damp. His mouth was whiney. Not very, but it turned down more than it turned up at the corners.

But Spid did not have time to study Norman's face before two or three other boys banged down their bicycles on the patio outside and came into the shed.

'We can practise in here,' Norman was saying. 'If we shut the door it won't disturb anybody, and Mum won't create. Have you got the drums, Mickey? And the trumpet, Dave? You have the mouth organ, Wally, and I'll have the guitar.'

Before Spid knew what was happening Norman dived down the side of the shed and hauled out a guitar case, to the side of which the spider was clinging with all its eight feet at once.

'Look at that, now!' Norman said in amazement. 'Did you ever see such a whopper? I bet it's bigger than the one down at Pratts that Mum is always yattering about. It belongs to the old gentleman, or else to Henry, I don't know which . . . .'

'Look at its eyes,' said the boy called Wally. 'And all those great furry legs! Do you suppose it bites, like those foreign jobs?'

'No!' Norman said decidedly. 'It's not a bit like the ones on telly. It's a British spider, aren't you, spider-boy?'

'That's right,' said Spid, feeling nervous, but anxious to brave it out.

'And you don't bite, do you?' said Norman, giving him a gentle poke.

'That's right, I don't,' said Spid again.

'Well then,' said Norman. 'What's your name, spider-boy? You're not Henry's spider, are you?'

'My name's Spid. And yes, I am Henry's spider,' said Spid, retreating into the shadows, but the boys pounced on him.

'Hold him, Wally!' Norman cried. 'And watch out! Somebody's coming!'

The door was flung open, and Norman's sister Linda appeared.

'Oh, Norm! Are you going to practise? Do let me be in the band,' she pleaded.

'You haven't got anything to play,' they told her crossly. Linda, they thought, was much too young to be in their group that they called the Swinging Satellites. She couldn't even keep time.

53

'I've got a comb,' Linda pleaded. 'And lots of loo paper! I can play as well as you can!'

They turned their backs on her. Linda begged, and finally cried, and then begged again, and they could not get rid of her.

Spid was feeling rather sorry for Linda when Norman said suddenly and firmly: 'Look here, Lin! You won't like it out here, you know you won't! There's spiders!'

He opened his fist and Spid charged out, incensed by the tight, hot palm and the tight prison of Norman's fingers. 'Isn't he a nice little chap, then?'

Linda let out a shriek that would have stopped a train.

'Aie . . eee! How horrible! Oh the nasty thing! Throw it out and stamp on it!' she cried, flying back to the house as if a regiment of spiders was on her heels.

'There you are!' said Norman. 'Now we'll have some peace and quiet!' And for safety's sake he shut up Spid inside the guitar case, when he had removed the guitar.

The boys began to play some moderately proficient music. Norman was by far the most practised performer of the group. He could sing too, and as the little band played on Spid danced and jiggled inside the case, and wished he were outside where he had room to dance properly, and even to sing with the group.

There came a nasty crack! and one of the guitar strings snapped.

'There!' Norman exclaimed. 'That's done it—

unless I've got another one . . . .'

He opened the guitar case, and dived inside. Spid ran out and sat on one end of the guitar while the boys rootled and grumbled and grumbled and rootled.

'You said you would get a spare one,' the others accused Norman, and they continued to blame him when he went off to the house to search in his bedroom.

'Never thinks ahead, does Norm! Now we can't play the full band! And tomorrow it's cadets and then it's Sunday! He's just *thick*, is old Norm!'

While they grumbled, Spid ran up and down the guitar spinning a thread which was every bit as strong and durable as the broken one.

He had just finished it when Norman came back from the house looking crestfallen.

'I thought I had one,' he muttered, picking up the instrument and twanging it hopelessly. A beautiful note came from the string, and then others, as Norman plucked at them in astonishment.

'Gee!' Norman whispered. 'It's mended!'

'It's the perishing spider!' Wally remarked. 'It was climbing up and down the thing while you were away.'

'What, *you*?' Norman said, addressing Spid.

'That's right,' said Spid, as modestly as he could.

'Why, you clever little devil!' Norman said gratefully. 'Thanks a lot!'

He began to play, and the rest joined in.

Spid danced joyously on the floor. He whipped his threads into crazy patterns, and turned them inside out in a kind of frenzy, as the boys' music grew wilder and wilder.

Linda came and peeped through the keyhole, and then rushed shrieking to her mother.

'Mum! Mum! The boys have got a huge spider in there, and the shed is full of cobwebs! You ought to go and tell them off!'

Mrs Gridley came striding out of the house.

She flung open the door of the shed, and the look on her face frightened even Spid, who fled underneath a little bench and pretended he wasn't there.

The other boys were sent home. Norman was provided with a duster and told to clear the shed of cobwebs before he came in to have his tea.

Later on, he came back to look for Spid, who was still trying to make up his mind whether to go home that same night, or to stay where he was and teach the Pratt family a lesson. He would have liked to have a friendly word with Mrs Gridley, but something told him she would not be quite so hospitable in her own house. Spiders were one thing, and cobwebs were another. (But without cobwebs there would be no spiders. Not even a Spid.)

Much to his surprise he caught a fat fly that had been stunned by Norman's flapping duster. Having finished it he decided to spend the night where he was after all. He was quite content to sleep inside the guitar case, when Norman offered it to him as a bedroom.

# 8

# The Flood

Up the road, the Pratts were turning the place upside down looking for Spid. Grandpa had come back to spend a day.

Henry called, Grandpa bellowed, Mrs Pratt coaxed and chirruped. Mr Pratt, much annoyed by the fuss, went out. The coal cellar was turned completely inside out, and every lump of coal dumped outside in the yard. Then it was all dumped back inside again.

'Utterly selfish, like all animals!' Grandpa roared. 'Knows I can't get up without him!' But he stamped from room to room pounding cushions, slamming cupboard doors and desk lids, sitting down to puff and grumble and bouncing up again to rummage and search as if his stiff knees had never been heard of.

They all went to bed in the worst of tempers, though Henry's mood was tinged with deep despair. If Grandpa could not find Spid, if his mother could not, and his father knew nothing about it, then something quite terrible and final must have happened to his spider.

He looked down the wastepipe for the fiftieth time, but saw no cobwebs, nor the faintest vestige of a sign of Spid. Henry resigned himself to thinking he would never see him again.

And when it began to rain that night he abandoned all hope. Spiders do not like rain. They take refuge in drainpipes and get washed away. They drown very quickly, partly through fear. And as it rained and rained and rained and *rained*, Henry told himself that Spid could not possibly have survived the downpour.

But down the road Spid was still safe and dry inside the guitar case, although the shed was rapidly filling with water pouring off the patio, and presently the case began to float around the place like a little boat.

Not far away down the road the river was rising inch by inch, while everyone slept and the rain kept raining. The drains and ditches filled and overflowed, and so did the river. By morning it was in the garden and the house was surrounded, halfway up the front door.

The guitar case floated out of the shed window, into a wide, flowing river, and Spid did not know where it was taking him until there came a considerable bump! as it struck the side of the house, just hard enough to raise the lid an inch or so, and Spid scrambled out.

Daylight was coming, and he was dazzled by the stretches of water, out of which the fences and garden sheds stuck like almonds on a trifle pudding. The water was still gently moving and rising.

The guitar case made a very good boat, but Spid did not want to be carried away to nowhere. He made a frantic leap and clung to the ivy on the side of Mrs Gridley's house.

It was still raining—a very disagreeable morning in fact. There was nothing for him to perch on down below, so he climbed upwards, and did not stop until he came to a bedroom window and crept inside.

It was good to be safe and dry again. Since it began to rain he had not felt at all secure inside the shed, and certainly not inside that stuffy box. Stuffy places that one chooses to be in are one thing, but stuffy places that one does not choose are quite another.

He shook himself and sneezed, not loudly, but loud enough to wake the sleeper in the bed inside the bedroom.

The sleeper sat up and screamed. And it was Norman's sister Linda.

'Ow . . . w . . . w . . . ww. . . owwww!' Linda yelled. 'There's a spider in my room! There's a spider!'

Norman heard her in his room next door.

He leapt out of bed and burst into his sister's bedroom. But it was not Spid who took his attention, it was the floodwater outside, rapidly covering the garden and mounting up the walls of the house.

'Mum! Mum!' he yelled, rushing down the passage. 'There's a flood! There's a flood!'

'Norm! Norm! Don't leave me with the spider!' shrieked Linda, but Norman was much too excited to take any notice of her cries.

He roused his mother, who put on her dressing-gown and stood looking down in horror at the hall below, which was already awash, as was the kitchen beyond. And even while they watched the water lapped at the lower stairs.

Norman rushed down splashing across the hall for his gumboots. Mrs Gridley hastily got dressed. Linda went on screaming about the spider.

Spid tried to make himself as small as possible, but with gumboots trampling and the water rising outside there was such a commotion he was terrified of being trodden on.

'There's a *spider*!' yelled Linda.

'Hush, Lin! Don't make that silly noise!' her mother called from her bedroom. 'Get up and get dressed at once! Put your warm clothes on—there's a *flood*! Never mind about spiders!'

'I'm going to get Mr Barlow's boat,' shouted Norman, wrenching open the front door. The water surged in, but before his mother could stop him Norman was gone.

Mrs Gridley wondered if she had time to make a pot of tea before the water reached the electricity, and whether it was dangerous to put the kettle on. Perhaps she might be able to find the paraffin stove and balance it on the kitchen dresser or take it upstairs.

The water came up to the tops of her gumboots. With great difficulty she climbed on a chair and lit the stove. The kettle fussed into life, and she reached for the teabags from the dresser. No milk, but never mind. The larder was well under water by now, but a cup of tea would be so welcome, and probably it would settle Linda, who was always making a fuss about spiders, and probably the sight of the flood had upset her too.

'I'm coming, Lin,' she called, thankful that Linda had stopped screaming, but as she trod gingerly forward the chair tipped up underneath her, the teapot fell with a crash, and she collapsed into the floodwater, striking her head against the corner of the kitchen table.

Mrs Gridley was knocked out, as they say, and she remained unconscious for nearly a quarter of an hour, during which time the water rose and rose. Partly propped up by the table she was saved from drowning by her head being held clear of the water as it mounted, and she came round to see Norman's face leaning anxiously over her as he leaned in through the kitchen window, and said: 'Mum! Mum! Are you all right?'

There was a neighbour at his shoulder, who now clambered inside and between them they hauled out Mrs Gridley and put her in the boat.

'Mr Davis has gone for Linda at the back,' Norman announced, 'but I'll just go up and see if he's got her.'

He climbed back into the room and up the stairs. Linda's room was empty. Outside, people with boats were rescuing other people through windows, and rowing them away to safe places.

The water rose and rose.

'They've taken her,' Norman said, climbing outside again. 'I bet they've got her in the village hall. It's high up. Come on!'

Mrs Gridley was suffering from shock and the coldness of the water. The neighbour said they ought to take her straight to the hospital. They rowed down the street as far as the end, and then up the Promenade, level with the first-floor shop windows. It was a most peculiar sensation.

And meanwhile Linda, getting no answer to her cries, and being too frightened of the water to go down, and of the spider to stay where she was, fled up the attic stairs into the attic and sat clinging to the window-sill in her nightdress, past crying, past screaming, and almost past any hope of being rescued.

She could not imagine why Norman had deserted her, nor why her mother did not reply, nor why they had both left her alone with the horrible spider and the terrible flood.

Spid followed behind her at a respectful distance. He did not want to be drowned either, and he saw no reason why they should just stay there in Linda's bedroom and be forgotten.

Besides, he was a little nervous that Linda might do something silly in her terror, and even perhaps fall out of the window into the water outside.

So he stayed on the far side of the attic and tried to calm her down.

'I can't think why you are so frightened of spiders, Linda,' he said reproachfully. 'We have never done you any harm.'

'*Ugh!*' said Linda, shuddering. 'I *hate* them!'

'*Why* don't you like us?' Spid asked plaintively.

'It's . . . all . . . those . . . legs!' burst out Linda. 'And . . . and the way you *walk*!'

'Sorry,' said Spid. He was quiet for a time.

'Oh why don't they come?' moaned Linda.

'They don't know you are here,' Spid said sagely. 'Perhaps they think you have been rescued—or just drowned!'

'Oh no—oo!' sobbed Linda.

'Well,' said Spid. 'I expect they've just got everybody out of the houses, in boats, and have gone away.'

'Oh no—oo—oo!' wailed Linda.

'They may come back if they can't find you,' said Spid comfortingly.

It was very quiet. The voices of the rescuers that had echoed for a short while below were now long out of hearing. Only the rain pattered on the leads outside and splashed in through the attic window.

'If you would care to move across the sill a little I could take a peep outside,' said Spid. 'There may be something we can do, or some way of drawing attention to ourselves. You can shout, of course, but nobody took much notice when you did it before.'

'I know,' sobbed Linda, edging away from the window when she saw Spid coming.

He climbed on to the window frame and looked down.

The water was rising all the time. And down below, on a level with the bedroom windows, a table had come floating down the street upside down, and was gently knocking against the side of the house.

It would make a very good boat, Spid thought.

'Look!' he said. 'You take a peek over the edge.

There's a table there, just waiting to become a boat! If you get into it, it will soon float away, and somebody will see you. Isn't that a good idea?'

Linda crept to the window keeping one eye on Spid, who was spinning a kind of net at the end of a long thread.

'I'll never get down there,' she whimpered.

'Oh yes you will,' Spid said, 'because I will help you. Just get in this net and hold tight and I'll let you down!'

Bravely Linda climbed over the sill and sat in the net. Suddenly she felt she could trust Spid. He was not in the least like an ordinary spider.

The table was still bobbing on the water just below. Spid let her down slowly, slowly, on the end of the web, till she touched the table and stepped into it. It tipped a little, and she sat down suddenly, looking up at the small, round body of the spider, clinging to the window-sill with all its eight legs, and now beginning to wind in the thread.

'Don't push off just yet,' Spid called down to her, 'I'll get you some oars.'

He went back into the attic, and presently two straight slats of wood were lowered on to the table by the thread. They would make very fine oars.

Linda looked up at the little spider on the window-sill, slowly winding his empty thread aloft.

'Are you going to stay there?' she asked doubtfully.

He looked so small and helpless from below, and the water was rising so fast. If it rose as far as the attic Spid

might be drowned.

'Oh yes,' Spid said, 'I shall stay here until the flood goes down. There are plenty of flies to eat in these old dusty corners. Goodbye, dear! Take great care, don't try to stand up or do anything foolish! Give my regards to your family! Safe journey! Goodbye!'

'Oh spider, do come too!' begged Linda, clinging to the ivy on the side of the house. 'Please come with me! Please do! I don't want you to be drowned, and I'm not a bit afraid of you any more!'

'Oh well, if you insist, dear,' said Spid, happily.

He slid down the thread in a minute, and let Linda row him, rather clumsily, round the side of the house and into the village street.

# 9
## Rescue from the Flood

Norman, having seen his mother into hospital, rowed Mr Barlow's boat to the village hall in search of Linda. She was not there.

Quite horrified at not finding her, he set off again for his own house, accompanied by Henry, who had arrived with his family a short while before Norman did.

They rowed down the street, and met Linda paddling along on her upturned table, which was beginning to leak.

'There's our kid!' Norman shouted, waving an oar.

Henry waved too. Linda gave them a cool flap of her hand. She still resented Norman leaving the house without her.

'Come on! Climb in!' her brother ordered her, offering his hand, while Henry steadied the boat, which was bumping against the table. Linda scrambled aboard without thanking him. The table began to float away.

'Wait!' Henry shouted, leaning out over the water. 'There's my spider in it! There's Spid!'

'It's *my* spider!' cried Linda. 'It rescued me out of the attic! It spun a rope and let me down on to the table when you left me to drown!'

'It's *my* spider!' Norman claimed hotly. 'It has been in our shed for days! Don't start being funny about it belonging to you! How else do you think it got on to the table?'

'I brought it!' shrieked Linda. 'It saved me! I told you it did!'

'Why, you *hate* spiders!' jeered Norman. 'You run a mile when you see one coming! I never heard anyone scream like you did when I showed you this fellow of mine in the shed last night!'

'You stole it from *me*,' broke in Henry. 'It belongs to our house. You ask your mother if it doesn't.'

'Where is Mum?' wailed Linda. 'She'll tell you it's my spider if I say so. You see!'

'She'll tell you it's *my* spider,' Henry interrupted. 'Why, she knows I've had it for weeks till you pinched it!'

'I never pinched it!' shouted Norman.

'It came to help *me*,' sobbed Linda.

The table with Spid on it was rapidly parting company with the boat that had the children in it, and was floating away down the flooded street.

'Get it, quick!' shouted Henry, snatching the oars from Norman. Norman grabbed at them, Linda was caught in between and knocked off her feet. She lay howling on the planks.

Still fighting for the oars Henry managed to turn the boat round, but Norman turned it back again, and they twirled and spun in the middle of the floodwater till the sound of a motorboat's engines stopped their battle for a brief moment, and a larger boat manned by several

69

neighbours drew up alongside them.

'Come on, then! You're quite safe now!' the man in charge hailed them. 'Give us the little one! Don't cry, love! We'll have you back in the village hall in two shakes! They've got hot drinks in there, and we'll find your mum!'

'Mum's in hospital,' Norman grunted. Linda set up a fresh howl.

'Eh? What happened then?' said their rescuer, as kind hands reached over the gunwale and lifted Linda into the motorboat.

'Come on, son! Jump to it! We'll take the boat in tow . . . ' said the skipper. 'Never mind about the table. We'll rescue all the furniture later on when we have got the people out. Hurry up, you two! Pass up the painter! We'll need all these boats from now on. No mucking about, please!'

Another hand reached over and seized the rope hanging in the bows of Mr Barlow's boat.

Ignominiously the boys found themselves being towed back to the village hall, where Mr Barlow quickly reclaimed his craft, and far away down the flooded street Spid floated quietly out of sight.

# 10

## With Aunty Bloss

The table came to rest in a small backwater, bumping quietly against a flight of brick steps. The ground was higher now, the street was climbing up a hill, on the sides of which the houses stood high and dry.

No sooner had it reached dry land than Spid scuttled down one of the legs, ran across the grass and up the brick path to the nearest shelter he could find, which happened to be underneath the door of the house belonging to the grass and the brick path and the steps below.

'Peace and quiet,' thought Spid. 'It isn't much to ask, just a little peace and quiet. Nobody wants to be fought about and argued over, certainly not by tiresome children. Popular! Oh yes, that's me! But on my own terms, thank you! And keeping my dignity, please! Being friends, yes, but not a *pet* to anybody . . . oh no!'

He was damp and cold, and not a little frightened by the flood water, and the helplessness of feeling himself afloat and far away from Henry's house. Now he looked around for some warmth and comfort, and found it on the other side of the door. A small passage led into a kitchen where there was a fire and a wool rug and some welcome dark corners, also a budgerigar in a cage. Nobody else at all.

''Allo,' said the budgerigar.

'Hello, birdie,' said Spid, running underneath

the rug.

'Who are you talking to, Boyboy?' said a voice. A lady came into the room. 'I thought I heard you say "hello" quite nicely,' she said to him.

''Allo, birdie,' said the budgerigar.

'Oh! That's a new word!' said his mistress, admiringly. 'I've never heard you say "birdie" before. Now say: "Hello, birdie." Not that nasty 'allo-'allo!'

''Allo! 'Allo! 'Allo, birdie!' replied the budgerigar.

'Oh you are naughty!' reproved his mistress. 'Just when I'm trying to teach you to talk like a little gentleman!'

''Allo! 'Allo! 'Allo!' repeated the budgerigar, bouncing up and down and spilling its seed on the carpet.

'Now look at that!' said its mistress patiently. 'Just when I've swept the room and made everything clean and tidy! Grandma's coming,' she told him, putting her face close to the bars. 'They've phoned up from the village hall, and she'll be here any minute. She'll tell you you are a naughty, untidy, common little bird. Why can't you say "hello" like the other budgies do?'

''Allo Granma!' cried the budgerigar joyously.

His mistress stooped down to pick up the rug and shake the seeds out of it. Spid ran out from under the rug and the lady gave a yell and dropped it. But before he could hide himself again she had seized a glass from the dresser and clamped it down on top of him. All his little dashes landed up against the solid round sides of a glass prison. The lady slipped a sheet of paper under-

72

neath the glass and deposited it triumphantly on the table next to the budgerigar's cage.

The little bird screamed in fright, but then began to laugh mockingly when he saw that Spid could not get out.

'There!' said his mistress. 'Did you ever see such a big spider before, Boyboy? *I* never did! We'll just wait till they bring Grandma from the village hall, and when she has had a peep at it I'll take it down the steps and tip it back in the water. It won't upset her when she sees it can't get out.'

'Naughty! Naughty! Naughty!' screamed the budgerigar.

'You be quiet!' said the lady. 'I'm going to put on the kettle for a cup of tea. They'll be here in a minute. I hope she won't be too upset by the flood. We're lucky, Boyboy, living in a higher part of the village.'

''Allo! 'Allo! 'Allo!' said the budgerigar. It hopped into the bottom of its cage and pressed its stubby beak against the bars, quite close to Spid, who did not know whether it wanted to be friendly or to bite him.

'Hello, birdie,' it said politely.

'There!' came its owner's voice. 'I knew you could speak nicely if you tried. Good Boyboy! Clever bird! You say that to Grandma and I daresay she'll give you some chocolate.'

''Allo! 'Allo! 'Allo!' shrieked the budgerigar.

It was attacking the door of its cage with its stubby beak, and while its mistress was getting out the teacups

73

and putting on the kettle to make the tea, it walked out.

Spid quailed a little as it waddled across the table towards him, but the moment it tipped the glass over the edge he escaped and ran for the nearest shelter, which was the cage.

The lady jumped round at the noise of the breaking glass, and the bird fled back the way it had come, while its mistress stood scolding it and bolting the door so it could not get out again. Spid crouched under the drinking-water container, wondering which was the best way to die—to be tossed into the river by an unfeeling lady, or pecked to pieces by a savage bird. Either way he was quite determined to fight to the end.

The lady busied herself in sweeping up the pieces of broken glass, but the budgerigar spied out Spid in an instant.

'Hello, hello,' it said agreeably. 'How are you, my dear?'

'Quite well, thank you, birdie,' said Spid, still crouching. He did not quite trust the beak behind those green and golden feathers though the little bird seemed friendly enough.

'Happy days!' said the budgerigar.

'Thank you, birdie,' said Spid.

The lady came over to stare at them in amazement.

'Is that *you* talking, Boyboy?' she asked.

'No lady, it's me—Spid, lady,' he replied.

''Allo, lovey,' chirped the bird.

'Not 'Allo!—Hell . . . o,' Spid corrected him.

'Hell . . . o, spider. Hell . . . o dear,' it pronounced primly. ''Appy happy, 'appy days! Amen!'

'Now look,' said Spid severely. 'You can do better than that, my lad! If you don't do what your mistress tells you I know somebody else who is going to take a swim in the river.'

'Ow!' said the bird, looking abashed.

'Leave him to me, lady,' said Spid. 'I'll have him talking properly in no time. Do you want him in English or in French?'

'Oh . . . English please,' said the lady looking startled.

The doorbell rang, and within seconds the room was filled from the back by two ambulancemen and a grandma.

'We brought the ambulance down the upper road,' one of the men explained, 'but the water is going down. There you are, Gran! You'll be all right now you're with your daughter. A nice cup of tea and a warm by the fire, and you'll be back again in your own home by bedtime! So long, love!'

The men went out, and Grandma sat down in a chair by the fire and panted.

'Three cups of tea I had at the hall,' she said. 'And each one nastier than the last. I don't think they've ever heard of a teabag! And they ran out of sugar before I got there. Thanks, dear, I'll take another lump. Where's Dick?'

'Oh, he's helping with the flood,' her daughter said.

'Getting people's furniture out and all that. Did the water come inside the house then, Mum?'

'Well, no,' Grandma admitted. 'But the Socials thought it might, so they came and got me out. My house stands a lot lower than yours. I don't know what I'll do if the water does get in. I've only just had the kitchen done out, and the front garden is ever so nice. I don't like to think of my geraniums all floating round in their pots. You've still got that silly bird, then?'

'Hello, Granma,' said the budgerigar politely.

'Well, that's quite nice,' said Grandma. 'You have been teaching it to speak properly, have you, Bloss?'

'Well . . . ' she hesitated, but before she could reply Grandma had caught sight of Spid trying to leave the cage through the bars. She gave an enormous gasp and fainted away.

Spid, now clear of the cage, ran to the tap to damp a tissue which he dragged to Grandma's face, tenderly mopping her forehead while her daughter held a cup of tea to her lips.

Slowly Grandma opened her eyes.

'Aiee . . . eee!' she shrieked on seeing Spid's round, anxious eyes peering into hers, and she fainted again.

'Oh do go away!' Bloss begged him. 'I'm sure you mean well, but it *won't do*! Grandma can't bear the sight of spiders. You see what it does to her. Just go away and hide yourself and don't come back any more!'

'I only wanted to be friends,' Spid murmured. He crept away very crestfallen, looking for a dark corner to

76

hide himself in, but just then he heard the budgerigar rasping its bill along the bars of its cage. It was inviting him to come back, and because he felt lonely and his feelings were rather hurt, Spid went.

The bird made room for him on its perch.

'Hello spider,' it announced.

Spid's heart felt warm and comforted. They cuddled up together, and nobody could see Spid for the bright breast feathers of the bird.

'How you can have great spiders like that running about in the house I can't imagine!' Grandma was whimpering, quite overcome by all the events of the morning.

'Oh I *don't*, Mum dear,' her daughter was soothing her. 'I think it must have come up the path out of the flood. And it isn't an ordinary spider, Mum. It's ever such a funny one. It is teaching Boyboy to speak properly. You know how rough he has been. Well, you ought to listen to him now!'

Inside the cage the bird and Spid were conversing quietly together.

'Not 'Ow are yer?' Spid was repeating. 'It doesn't sound nice. You should say: How-do-you-do?'

'How-de-do-de-do-de-do?' said the budgerigar.

'How-do-you-do?' repeated Spid patiently.

'Cocky-doodle-do!' giggled the budgerigar. 'He-he! Noisy boyser! Noice boysie! A silly old spider sat beside a . . . a . . . .'

'Say "How-do-you-do, Grandma?"' repeated Spid.

77

''Ow do! Yer doing' fine!' cackled the bird.

'Very well! I'm leaving you!' said Spid, but the bird began to shriek at the top of its voice: 'Don't go! Don't go! Stay with Boyboy! I loves yer! I loves yer!'

'Please don't go . . . I love you!' Spid repeated gently. There was a pause . . . then:

'Please don't go, spider! I love you!' said the bird in an altered voice.

'There!' said Bloss in triumph. 'Did you ever hear anything like it?'

'Well no, I never did,' said Grandma, staring. 'Where did you come from, Daddy-Long-Legs?'

'My name is Spid, lady,' he said courteously. I came down the flood on an upside-down table that floated. I belong to Henry Pratt.'

'To Henry Pratt?' exclaimed Grandma and Bloss together. 'Did you say to Henry Pratt?'

'Yes ma'am. Yes lady,' replied the spider.

'But Henry is my grandson!'

'But Henry is my nephew!' both ladies exclaimed together.

'Yes, ladies!' Spid agreed. 'Henry told me that his grandma fainted when she saw a spider, and that his Aunty Bloss shut them up in toothglasses . . . .'

'I really am very sorry,' said Aunty Bloss.

'If anyone had *told* me,' muttered Grandma.

'Naughty! Naughty! Naughty!' shrieked the budgerigar.

'Be quiet!' commanded Spid. The little bird turned

its back and tucked its head underneath its wing, muttering something rude.

The telephone bell rang and Aunty Bloss went to answer it.

'It's Henry's dad,' she announced on her return. 'He wants to know if we are all all right.'

'Yer doin' fine!' croaked the budgerigar.

'I *beg* your pardon?' said Spid.

'You are doing fine, dear!' peeped the bird, ending up with a cackle.

'You are very rude,' said Spid. 'And I'm leaving!'

'Oh sorry all! Sorry all!' cried the bird in great agitation. 'Gurk! Gurk! Beg yer pardon!'

Aunty Bloss got up and put a duster over the cage, but Spid was quicker still. Before the budgerigar could get back on to its perch he had tied up its bill with such a strong cobweb that it was not able to say another word for several hours.

# 11

## After the Flood

Spid was awakened by the sound of heavy footsteps.

Both ladies began talking at once to a man whom Spid recognised at once as Henry Pratt's father.

'You don't know what we've got here, John!' Aunty Bloss said to him, taking the cloth off the budgerigar's cage.

'What? That nutty bird?' he exclaimed. 'I've seen that before! Does it talk yet?'

The bird muttered something incoherent through the web that bound his bill, and Spid took the opportunity of making a dash for freedom. He ran out of the cage and down the fall of the tablecloth, but not before Mr Pratt had noticed him.

'Look out! There's a spider!' he cried, making a lunge at Spid with his foot.

'No—no! You mustn't!' shrieked Aunty Bloss. 'It isn't just any spider! It's Henry's spider! It came down with the flood!'

'Good heavens!' said Mr Pratt. '*That* one! Henry has been raising heaven and earth for the past few days, since he lost it. He blames *me*, I may tell you! He thinks I squashed it if you please! And he won't believe a word I say about it. Well, in that case I suppose I had better take it home with me.'

This time it was not a toothglass that Aunty Bloss popped on top of Spid, but a teacup, and a minute later he was transferred by Mr Pratt's large red hands into Mr Pratt's large dark pocket, together with a handkerchief, a box of matches, and a number of coins pressed down on top of him.

The stuffiness of the pocket and the mixed smells of tobacco and motor oil became as much as he could bear. He thought he really would soon die of a very unpleasant kind of suffocation, before he could ever see Henry again.

As Mr Pratt left Aunty Bloss's house to go home, and fortunately for Spid, he suddenly gave a gigantic sneeze, and put his hand in his pocket to find his handkerchief.

As he pulled it out, Spid came too. He dropped on to the pavement and ran to hide himself in a crack among the paving stones, where he crouched until Mr Pratt had walked out of sight.

Much later in the evening he found himself once more outside Henry's garden gate, but of Henry there was not a sign to be seen.

Everything was wet and uncomfortable and unpleasant after the flood, and there was no welcome anywhere for Spid.

He hung around, cold and wretched, till someone opened a window, leaving a few inches open at the top. Spid climbed up and let himself down inside on a long thread that would have disgusted Mrs Gridley. Nobody was around in the cold bedroom but downstairs the familiar warmth and comfort of the kitchen came out to meet him. He scuttled down the stairs and under the kitchen door, to find the family sitting at tea.

Henry's father was explaining how sure he was that Henry's spider was in his pocket, till it had escaped half way home, and Henry, very sober, was trying to reconcile himself to the fact that he had very nearly had a spider again, but not quite, while Mrs Pratt was making comforting noises to them both, and assuring them that sooner or later Spid was simply bound to turn up again.

'He won't,' said Henry.

'Oh, he *will*!' said Henry's mother.

Henry's father said nothing.

Spid climbed up the back of Henry's chair, walked on to his shoulder, and crept round his neck.

'Ugh!' said Henry, scratching.

'Henry! It's there! It's THERE! Your spider!' cried his mother excitedly.

'Well I'm blowed!' said his father. 'I don't believe it ever left my pocket after all! The cunning fellow! I expect he had a good strong thread to climb back with, so I never knew.'

'Don't tell Mrs Gridley, or she'll tell Norman,' Henry pleaded. 'He'll steal it if he can, and so will that Linda! Mrs Gridley knows Spid is mine anyway!'

'I'm not anybody's. I'm ME!' Spid was muttering to himself, on Henry's knee. 'Friends—yes! Best friends if you like, lots of friends, and eight handshakes all round, but spiders are free people, they don't *belong* to anybody. Besides, they laughed at me once,' Spid reminded himself, when he had got used to feeling warm and wanted again. 'I shall stay here just as long as I want to, and as long as they are good to me. Henry is nice, his mother is nice, his grandpa is quite nice, his father is not very nice, his Aunty Bloss is fairly nice, his grandma is only a bit nice, his father is horrid. He'd like to squash me if it wasn't for Henry, I know he would. I shall pay him out!' Spid said to himself. 'He's lucky to have a spider like me about the place, and not a budgerigar like that silly little bird of Aunty Bloss's. Tonight when he's asleep I'll take my Big Revenge!' thought Spid, becoming more and more fierce and determined as he ruminated.

Spid slept in Henry's room, but it was easy enough for a spider to slip in and out under the crack. When everyone in the household had gone to bed, he marched out purposefully into the corridor.

Mr Pratt liked to leave his clothes in the bathroom, all ready to put on in the morning. Spid spent a considerable time weaving threads round the trouser legs and the sleeves, so that without a pair of scissors nobody could possibly get into them.

All the time he spun he muttered: 'Spoiling my night's rest . . . just because I have eight legs, and pretty good ones too!' He was creating such an under-current to his toil that at first he did not notice a creak on the stairs, following a very slight tinkle down below, as if someone were opening the silver drawer.

84

When he did notice it Spid stopped grumbling and went to the bathroom door.

All was quiet in the bedrooms. Henry slept, his father slept, his mother slept, there was not a movement, not even a snore. But down below something or someone was moving about, and very, very quietly coming up the stairs.

Spid crept on to the landing, and saw a completely unknown figure making his way upwards with socks over his shoes, gloves on his hands, and a cap pulled down over his face.

'I don't think he's very nice,' thought Spid. 'I don't think he's nice at all! I think he's going to steal Mrs Pratt's jewellery, and Mr Pratt's cufflinks, and put them in that bag I can see down there in the hall! I can't allow that,' said Spid, dashing to the top of the stairs.

The burglar was still only part of the way up. As quietly as possible Spid spun a thread across the fourth step from the top, and another on the very top stair.

But the second thread was not necessary, because the burglar caught his foot in the first, tripped, fell, swore, and clattered backwards down the stairs to lie breathless on his back in the hall.

Quick as a flash Spid was after him. Before the man could struggle to his feet he was bound from head to foot in strong cobwebs. By the time Mr Pratt had arrived on the scene there was nothing left for him to do but call the police and hand over the criminal to the law, caught completely red-handed, and secured a great deal more firmly than by any handcuffs.

'Spider!' said Mr Pratt, when they were all sitting round the kitchen fire and drinking cocoa, before going back to bed. 'Spider, I take off my hat to you! Shake hands, old pal! Shake hands!'

'Spid's the name, sir,' Spid said warmly. He shook Mr Pratt's hand with every one of his eight legs.

'Beautiful!' said Henry's mother, with tears in her eyes.

'And I'll tell you one thing, Mr Spid,' said Henry's father. 'I swear that for your sake I'll never, never, *never* tread on another spider in my life! Okay?'

'Just as you say, sir,' said Spid modestly.

Henry would have been utterly happy if it hadn't been for Norman. He felt certain that sooner or later his rival would make an attempt to get the spider back again, and when he did, he would not be likely to let it go.

Before going back to sleep Spid went into the bathroom and unpicked all the spider threads in Mr Pratt's trousers, and sleeves of his jacket and shirt. It took him half the night and he was deadly tired, but he felt it was the moment to let bygones be bygones.

# 12

## At Grandpa's

'You know, Grandpa does nothing but ask for that spider,' Mrs Pratt told Henry. 'I think it would be kind to let him have it for a little while. He found Spid so useful in pulling him up out of his chair.'

Henry said nothing, but he was thinking deeply. He had not slept soundly since the day of the flood, he was so afraid Norman and his friends might turn up at any minute and steal the spider. On Monday, Tuesday and Wednesday they had said as much at school. 'Just you wait, Henry!' they had threatened.

And Spid himself had not been very co-operative, since he thought it was unkind of Henry to keep him shut up all the long hours he was away at school. He thought it would be quite a change to go and spend a day with Grandpa. Henry agreed, because he thought Spid would be safer in Grandpa's house, and he would not have to worry about him all the time he was out.

'Everybody wants Spid,' he said to his mother. 'Even Mrs Gridley says nobody cleans the windows like Spid does.'

'Aunty Bloss would like to have him back too,' said Mrs Pratt. 'He is a most popular little fellow! Aunty Bloss says Boyboy has hardly spoken at all since the flood. At first she thought it was the shock of all that water, but now she thinks it is the spider he is missing. He got quite excited when its name was mentioned.'

87

'My two have gone daft about that insect,' said Mrs Gridley, 'and I suppose Norman has as much right to it as Henry has. It was in our house for days. And our Linda is breaking her heart to get it back again. She says it saved her life, so it has got to belong to her, and her only. We don't get any peace between the pair of them.'

'I suppose Henry did have it first,' said Mrs Pratt gently.

'That's right,' Mrs Gridley agreed, 'but it found its way to our house somehow, and my Norman says finding is keeping!'

Spid sat underneath the bath and listened.

He liked the feeling of popularity, but he did not enjoy being spoken of as any one person's property. Not even Henry's. He drummed his eight legs peevishly on the bath pipes till Mrs Pratt said something must be wrong with the plumbing, and if it went on she would have to send for the plumber.

When Mrs Gridley and Henry's mother were having cups of tea he appeared on the table in the middle of them.

'So there you are, spider!' said Mrs Gridley. 'We've been talking about you. Were you listening?'

'Yes,' said Spid, 'and I don't belong to Norman and I don't belong to Henry, and I don't belong to Linda, and I don't belong to Grandpa, and I don't belong to Aunty Bloss, and I don't belong to Henry's mum and dad, and I don't belong to you, Mrs Gridley!'

'Well then,' said Mrs Gridley, surprised, 'who do you belong to, then?'

'Just to me mostly,' said Spid. 'And I don't hold with being fought over, it is too noisy and rude. But I don't like being left alone either. I want to have interesting things happen to me all the time.'

'We can none of us have interesting things happen to us *all* the time,' Mrs Pratt admonished him. 'But it must be very dull living all day long under the bath. What would you like to do?'

'I'd like to spend different days with all the people who love me,' said Spid smugly. 'Just to take in turns.'

'Well that *is* a good idea!' said Mrs Gridley. 'And you can start with our Norman . . . .'

'No, start with Grandpa!' interrupted Mrs Pratt.

'No . . . Linda!' said Mrs Gridley.

'Aunty Bloss!' cried Mrs Pratt.

'There they go!' thought Spid, disgusted. 'Nobody asks *me* where I'd like to go! I'll make up my own mind!'

While the teacups were being rinsed he went outside to mend the clothes-line, and this being done he climbed over the fence and proceeded down the road to look for a welcome where he would best be appreciated.

Before long he became utterly, hopelessly and absolutely lost.

Every street looked like the one he had just left. Every shop looked like the shop where Mrs Pratt bought her groceries, or her greengroceries, or her odds and ends and bits and pieces. Every bank looked like the bank where she kept her money.

Spid knew, because he had once been out shopping with her, secretly, inside her shopping basket.

Even on that occasion he had been a little frightened, not only because of the parcels and paper bags dropping down so heavily on top of him, but also of the hazards of being seen and pounced on by other shoppers and their dogs and their children who stopped to speak to Mrs Pratt at one time or another during the morning. After all, the whole point of going out with her was to have a glimpse of the outside world, so hiding at the bottom of her basket among all the packages was hardly his idea of fun. He took to giving little hops and bounces, and in the end of course Mrs Pratt noticed him.

'Oh *Spid*,' was all she said, but he felt a little safer after that. Henry's mother would be sure to protect him if trouble arose. But instead, she forgot all about him, and squashed him flat underneath her library books. It took him the whole way home to wriggle free again.

Today there was no shopping basket and no Mrs Pratt to protect him, just miles and miles of pavements, all looking alike, and thousands of walking feet, all looking different. He hated the feet. Every pair of shoes, he felt convinced, was walking down the pavement for the sole purpose of squashing him flat, and no sooner had he escaped from one pair than another came marching . . . marching . . . marching . . . .

When it all became too much for his nerves he dived down a grating and found himself in a drain. Here there were flies, to be caught and eaten, and a large black beetle who told him that if he wanted to get anywhere in town he had better avoid the streets and use the sewers.

'Sewers?' exclaimed Spid. 'What's that?'

'Drains!' said the beetle simply. 'All pipes go into the sewers. You want to walk along the sewers and try all the pipes till you come to the address you are looking for. It's easy!'

It was not easy, but it was safer than using the streets.

Spid walked up miles of sewers and miles of drainpipes. There was nothing familiar about any of them. He became so tired that he had to take in turns, walking on six legs and resting two.

Finally he arrived at a drainpipe that had just the remotest echo of familiarity about it.

It was a bathwater outlet, but he had passed hundreds of those before. This one, however, had the faintest whiff about it that he recognised. It reminded him of somebody, but he was not sure who.

All the same he decided to explore it, and presently he found himself climbing up and up a wastepipe that led straight up into a bathroom.

It reminded him of the day he had found Henry (oh

Henry, why did I ever leave you? moaned Spid) but this pipe was longer and older, and actually had quite a lot of rough places on which to place, in turns, his eight climbing feet.

It was dark all the way up, and he soon lost sight of the dim light from the sewer below. He just went on climbing until he reached a kind of S-shaped pipe, on the further side of which somebody was having a bath.

'I knew it!' thought Spid in disgust. 'The moment they pull the plug out down I'll go! Soap suds, bath salts and all, and probably it will be much too hot as well. I'm not going to wait for that!'

Hastily he began to climb back the way he had come, but at that moment the person in the bath began to groan, and his groans turned into cries for help.

'I can't get out!' came a familiar voice, and the water thrashed about over Spid's head like a storm at sea beating on the rocks. 'I can't get out by myself!' roared Grandpa's voice. 'Oh where the devil is that spider?'

The voice died away in a wail of despair, though it was followed by a noise that was very like a bath tray being crashed several times on the side of the bath.

When this had quieted Spid stood upright on four of his legs and beat a tattoo with the other four on the bottom of the plug.

There came a terrified splashing, and then Grandpa's voice again: 'What's that? What the devil is happening? Who is busting up the bath?'

'It's me, Grandpa sir! It's me—Spid!' said Spid

urgently. 'Just wait for me to get out of this pipe, and I'll come and help you.'

'Hey there! Why, you fine little feller! You mighty top-notch little champion!' cried Grandpa, wallowing in the water above him. 'Just wait a moment, my beauty, and I'll have the plug out.'

'No, no, no!' urged Spid, clinging with all his eight feet to the pipe. 'I've got a better plan than that, sir, before you drown me! Just wait a moment while I climb up to the overflow outlet and I'll be with you before you can wink!'

Grandpa let out a crow of joy and lay quite still while Spid climbed up the pipe towards the circle of light shining through the overflow. It was blocked by Grandpa's ear. Grandpa had a phobia about sitting at the tap end of the bath.

'Move your head please, Grandpa sir,' Spid said, tickling Grandpa's lobe with a long, furry finger.

'Oh ... ow! Yes, of course! Sorry my boy!' said Grandpa.

Spid climbed through the outlet with some difficulty. He was a much bigger spider than when he had first come to live with Henry. He landed, finally, on the old gentleman's shoulder, amid a mountain of bubbles, for Grandpa liked to bathe in luxury, and never stinted himself when it came to bath oils and bubble baths.

Spid was rather dirty after a day's travelling in the sewers and up various drainpipes. He hastily washed himself in the froth, and then ran up the wall to the ceiling, where he let down a prodigious thread that Grandpa clasped, and hoisted himself out of the bath looking rather like a frosted Christmas ornament.

The water ran out with a roaring gush that would have taken the spider with it for many miles underground, and Spid shuddered a little as he climbed down and waited for Grandpa to dry himself.

'Perfectly simple,' Grandpa said. 'Nothing wrong with my legs. Just my knees that let me down. Always there when you are wanted, aren't you, Spiddy?'

'That's right, Grandpa sir,' said Spid agreeably.

With the old gentleman dry and dressed in a warm dressing-gown, the pair of them settled down in front of the fire to sip cocoa and digest flies respectively.

'How did you find me?' Grandpa wanted to know.

'Just taking a walk down the drain, Grandpa sir,' said Spid.

'Very intelligent! Very intelligent spider!' said Grandpa admiringly. 'I knew you would miss me. I was all for taking you home with me, but Henry's mum wouldn't hear of it. But you and I know best, don't we, Spiddy boy?'

'Yes, Grandpa sir,' said Spid, nodding off to sleep in front of the fire.

# 13

## At Linda's

In the morning Grandpa's home help came to clean his house, and Grandpa warned Spid to keep out of sight.

'She's a terror for spiders, is our Aggy!' said Grandpa. 'And so's the Meals-on-Wheels who comes at twelve. You had better get into the larder and stay there.'

The larder had no window, and was rather dark.

Spid was very angry at being shut up again in a place where there was not even a fly to stalk and play with. He spun a thick web to keep himself busy, and ate some of the Meals-on-Wheels trifle that Grandpa had not finished from the last call. He did not think much of it.

When the home help, and later on other callers had finished banging about in the house, Grandpa came to let him out, and suggested that they should go for a walk in the park.

'And today,' Grandpa said grandly, 'I shall hire a chair and sit in it underneath a tree, because when I want to get out you will be there to help me, won't you, Spid? And I shan't have all those people rushing to help me and calling me a poor old gentleman.'

'That's right, Grandpa sir,' said Spid.

They set out very slowly down the pavement, with Spid running alongside and Grandpa tapping with his stick, and closing every gate he passed that happened to be open.

Once a dog caught sight of Spid, and ran across the road to have a closer look at him, but quick as a flash Spid spun two loops of web round his muzzle, and they left him behind, frantically trying to rub himself free with his front paws.

'Got fleas,' Grandpa remarked complacently. 'Don't go near it, Spid! You'll catch them!'

They arrived at the gates of the park and walked across the grass to the chair-hire hut.

Grandpa was quite fussy about which chair he wanted to sit on, and when he had made his choice the chair attendant obligingly carried it over to the trees by the lake and set it down just where Grandpa told him to.

'Have a good sleep, sir,' he said, walking away.

'*Sleep*?' said Grandpa angrily. 'Who said I was going to sleep? I didn't hire a chair to go to sleep in. I can do that in my own bed.'

'That's right, Grandpa sir,' said Spid, who was watching the gnats dancing at the edge of the lake, and wondering whether they tasted good.

'Don't you run off and leave me, mind!' ordered Grandpa. 'I shall want you in a little while. I'll just rest my legs for a few minutes, and then we will stroll round the lake together.'

Spid settled down to being bored again, and in a few minutes Grandpa was fast asleep.

Spid strolled down to the edge of the lake and watched the gnats and the ducks and the waving reeds,

97

where the brighteyed minnows darted to and fro in the water. The idea came to him that while he waited for Grandpa to wake up he might do a little fishing.

It was a pity, he thought, that Grandpa could not share in the sport, but the old gentleman was comfortably asleep, and snoring too—so loudly that Spid did not notice approaching footsteps, until somebody ran down to the edge of the water close beside him, and with a gasp of astonishment a child's voice cried out: '*Spid!* It's Spid! Oh Spiddy, is it really you?'

Spid found himself snatched up, and gazing into the astonished eyes and the round pink cheeks of Norman Gridley's sister Linda.

He struggled and fussed and freed first one leg and then another, but Linda cupped him very firmly between her palms, and carried him away from the lake, crooning to him and coaxing him, while Grandpa slept on, quite innocent of the fact that now there would be no one to get him out of his chair.

'Oh Spid, don't you *know* me?' Linda reproached him. 'You saved my life, Spiddy, and you're my very own precious spider! You're not Norman's, and you're not Henry's, you are *mine*, and I'm going to keep you for ever and ever!'

Spid's heart sank at Linda's words, and her hot, clinging fingers. He would not have *bitten* her for all the world, but he came very near it when she began to run across the park to join her friends, who had all come into the recreation grounds to play on a

Saturday morning.

'I've found him! I've found my spider!' Linda cried, opening her fingers just far enough to display her prize.

Spid looked up into a sea of curious eyes and disapproving faces. 'Ugh! How horrible!' her friends said. 'Don't let it escape, Lin! It's a horrid great brute! Why don't you throw it in the lake?'

'It's my own darling pet spider!' Linda said indignantly. 'It saved my life, and I'm going to keep it for ever!' She flounced away from her friends and ran home across the park, with Spid bouncing about in her palm, wondering how soon he would be able to escape from her. When he did, he meant to find his way straight back to the park to rescue Grandpa, who had no business to go off to sleep and allow him to be kidnapped by this tiresome little girl.

He tried to look out between her fingers, so that he could make a note of the roads they passed, but Linda held him so tightly imprisoned that he could not see anything at all.

Poor Grandpa! Perhaps the chair attendant would help him when he wanted to get up and go home. He was a tiresome old gentleman, but not nearly so tiresome as this Linda.

After about ten minutes Linda arrived at her own house. She flew up the stairs and shut Spid inside the dolls' house.

That was fine, he thought at first, greatly relieved to be released from her hot and sticky fist, and pleased too

99

to find that the dolls' house had windows and a front door, so that surely he would be able to come and go as he pleased.

But the windows did not open, and the front door was glued shut. It was just another prison, though slightly more attractive than the last.

Spid wandered from one room to another, waiting for Linda to come back to him, but she had gone downstairs to have her dinner. She did not reappear until half an hour later, by which time he had had quite a comfortable sleep in an armchair in front of the little cardboard fire.

Linda shut and locked the door of her bedroom.

'I'm not having Norman coming in here,' she said, flinging open the front of the dolls' house. '*Now* Spid! Oh aren't you handsome and splendid? I thought I hated spiders, but I never knew one so beautiful as you are before!'

'Thank you, lovey,' said Spid modestly. He felt more kindly towards Linda, but the next moment she added:

'I'm going to see whether any of my dolly's clothes will fit you. I've got the most gorgeous little lacy bonnet!'

Spid recoiled in horror, but she seized him, and with her other hand opened a drawer full of dolls' clothes.

Out came a tiny pair of boots, and a miniature baby's cap, which she put on his body and tied under his stomach with pink ribbons. Spid crumpled himself up in shame and misery, but Linda smoothed out his unwilling legs, put the boots on two of them, and carried him over to her dressing-table mirror.

'Now look at yourself, precious,' she crooned. 'The biggest, the best, the most beautiful spider that ever was in the whole wide world! Don't you look lovely, then? Aren't you pleased with yourself, Spiddy spider?'

For answer, Spid screwed up his eyes and turned his head away from the looking glass. He could hardly bear to come face to face with such humiliation.

'Eight legs, and only two little boots,' Linda was murmuring. 'I'm going to knit you some little leg-warmers, beauty-boy, on teeny tiny needles. Probably I'll knit them on hairpins! Eight leg-warmers! All different—wouldn't you like that, Spiddy?'

'No,' said Spid in muffled tones.

'Oh Spid! Can't you be grateful? Then I'll knit you a scarf, shall I? In nice bright colours. Then I won't lose sight of you when I take you outdoors. I'll take you out in the park, Spiddy, in the dolls' pram, because if I let you run about on the grass I might not know where you are.'

Spid shuddered all over, but at that moment he heard sounds down below that slightly raised his spirits. Out in the shed the Swinging Satellites, led by Norman, were striking up a tune, and getting under way for some practice. Spid began to jiggle.

'Oh, Spid, you do look so funny jiggling like that,' giggled Linda. 'Your bonnet is all over your eyes. Do

102

let me get it straight. There, I'll tie your bow again!
You really are the most beautiful, the bravest, and the
best spider I ever saw in my whole life! Do you love me,
Spid?'

'No, I don't!' said Spid, jiggling away

'Oh, *Spid*!' Linda reproached him. 'Not a little bit?'

'No, not a little bit,' said Spid.

'All right! I don't love you either!' said Linda in a
rage. 'And you shan't wear that pretty bonnet, because
you don't deserve it. You're just a common, dirty little
spider!'

'No, I'm not,' said Spid, offended, but she whipped
the bonnet off him and shut him up again inside the
dolls' house.

Spid could not hear the music any longer.

Angrily he spun cobwebs so thickly all over the
inside of the dolls' house that it took Linda nearly a
week to clean it out again.

Linda ran downstairs to her piano practice, and Spid
could hear her pounding away on the keys, trying to
outdo the efforts of the boys in the garden shed. Her
angry strumming did not stir him like the music of the
Satellites, and although he did not like Norman he
disliked Linda even more.

# 14
## With the Group

When Linda had been playing the same piece of music for twenty minutes it suddenly stopped. There came sounds of protest and argument from down below, and shortly afterwards Linda came crying up the stairs, pursued by her mother.

It seemed that she had lost the key of her music-case, and Mrs Gridley was insisting that she should look for it until she found it. She was following Linda to make sure that she really did look for the key instead of sitting on the edge of her bed and pretending that she had.

'Have you looked in the bathroom?'

'Yes, Mum!'

'Have you looked in your clean clothes drawer?'

'YES, Mum!'

'Have you looked in your coat pocket?'

'YES, Mum! I HAVE, Mum!'

'I expect it's in your old dolls' house,' said Mrs Gridley, charging across the room and opening the dolls' house door.

Spid did not wait to be discovered. He dashed out under Mrs Gridley's feet, making her jump and scream in spite of herself.

'Oh that dreadful spider! Wherever shall we find it next? Catch it quick, Linda! We must tell Henry!'

'It's not Henry's,' said Linda, pouncing, but Spid

shot through her fingers and down the stairs. Mrs Gridley and Linda were still looking for him on the landing when he dropped down two flights, snatched his thread after him, and made for the open door. He had just crossed the sill when Norman came charging through, demanding a bottle of coke for his performers.

Spid changed course, rather than be squashed under Norman's feet, and scuttled into the garden shed, where the other Satellites sat, idly strumming on their instruments.

He was greeted by a burst of applause.

'It's the spider!'

'It's Norman's dancing spider come back!'

'Hi, Spiddy! Couldn't you do without us then, old mate?'

Spid turned to flee, but now here was Norman with the bottle of coke, and he was even better pleased to see Spid than his friends had been.

'Hello there, big fellow! Glad to see you! Just you listen to the music we've got ready for you! Come on, lads, let's give him a tune!'

The Satellites began to play.

Spid could not help it. All his eight legs twitched at once. His head and body began to gyrate in time to the music. The next minute he was whirling madly about the floor, legs flying in all directions.

The group was delighted beyond measure.

'We'll take him with us to the disco,' one of them

suggested. 'He'll be a sensation.'

'Not looking like that,' Norman said. 'Nobody will see him in all those flashing lights. We'll have to put some luminous paint on him.'

Spid noticed that all the boys were dressed in odd and gaudy costumes, tight-fitting and shiny. As the afternoon light faded, the spangles and sequins glittered in the twilight.

'He could get trodden on if we don't,' somebody suggested, and it was this remark that persuaded Spid to allow himself to be daubed with luminous paint, and decorated with sparkling sequins. It was not only better than a dolls' bonnet, but it made him feel quite pleased with himself.

'Do you mind if we paint your legs too, Spid?' asked Norman.

'That's okay,' said Spid, obligingly holding out first one leg and then another . . . .

'And what about his thread?' another boy asked. 'If it isn't shiny somebody might walk straight through it and bust it . . . .'

'Paint it! Paint it!' urged Spid. He spun out a long length of thread, and this in turn was painted gold and white and scarlet in sections. Spid re-wound it ready for use when needed.

'Am I a Satellite too, now?' he asked hopefully.

'Yes, of course you are! Well—no, you aren't!' Norman said excitedly: 'Boys, I've got an idea! We won't call ourselves the Satellites after all—we'll be the Spiders!'

The rest of the group were enthusiastic about the new name. Spid swelled with pride. They were all congratulating themselves when there came a battering on the door of the shed.

It was Linda, of course.

'Norm! Norm! You've got my spider! I know you've got my spider! Let me in!'

Spid immediately curled into a tight ball and hid underneath a stool. All the boys faced Linda angrily as she opened the door.

'Get out! You can't come in here! Keep away! Take your nose out of our affairs! No girls allowed in here! Leave us alone! Don't push in where you're not wanted! Scram! Go away! Go and lose yourself!'

'First you say I've got your key, and now it's your spider!' jeered Norman. 'You just want to get into the group, don't you? But it won't work. Belt up—see? We aren't having any girls in here.'

'I *know* you've got my spider,' Linda wailed, as the door was banged in her face. 'I put him in the dolls' house, and he ran away, and I know he came in here.'

The group began to play loudly, to drown her cries.

Spid uncurled himself. He could not resist the music and the next moment he had hung his new, splendid, coloured thread from the ceiling, and was dancing and gyrating like a madman on the end of it.

This, thought Spid, is life, and I have a whole group named after me! I am ME, Spid, the famous spider!

There came a piercing wail from the far side of the door, where Linda was peering through the keyhole. It was loud enough to penetrate the music.

'You *have* got my spider! SPID! Oh my darling Spid! What have they done to you? Oh Mum! Mum! MUM! Norman has got my spider!'

Linda's cries died away. Her footsteps retreated, and the group came to an abrupt halt.

'Time we left,' Norman said tersely. 'If she fetches Mum there could be trouble. Let's get down to the disco and practise there.'

In less than no time bicycles were pulled out of the shadows, instruments hurled into boxes and bags. Spid was gently introduced into a cardboard container and tied on to a bicycle carrier.

The whole group left the shed at a gallop, and hurled themselves down the street, pedalling madly.

Rather breathless, but not unduly worried, Spid travelled with them, winding in his coloured thread as he went.

Their destination was a kind of sports hall, a mile or two away. It was dimly illumined, but already another group of boys was there, tinkering with coloured lights. They were not pleased at the early arrival of Norman's group, but became interested when the story was unfolded, and Spid was displayed. For the next half hour he was the centre of attention, as light after light was tried out and played upon him. His portrait was being hastily pinned on to a large poster, destined to replace the one already hanging up outside, which announced to the public: 'Satellites play tonight! Meet Spid, the Dancing Star Spider!' And there he was in the middle of it, twenty times larger than life.

'I am the dancing Star Spider!' said Spid to himself, very well satisfied.

He tried not to think about Grandpa, still sitting in his chair by the lake, in the dark, perhaps . . . . But I couldn't help it, Spid thought, any more than it was my fault that Linda cried. She should never have dressed me up in those silly dolls' clothes, he said to himself angrily. I just wish Aunty Bloss's Boyboy could see me now!

The lights were fixed, and everybody trooped out to get hamburgers before the evening show. Spid was left in Norman's guitar case, but gradually he became aware that he too was hungry. Very hungry.

Norman had not thought of closing the case. After all, Spid was part of the group now. Anyone could see he did not want to leave them.

'You take a good rest before we begin, old mate,' Norman said. 'We shan't be long.'

'Okay, pal,' said Spid, curling up for a sleep.

But hunger woke him. The thought of the boys stuffing themselves with hamburgers while he was starving was more than he could bear. He wriggled out of the case and began to look about him.

The hall looked quite hopeful, in fact very.

There was plenty of dust round the windows, and in

the beams of the ceiling. Where there was dust there were flies—flies alive, flies gone to sleep for the winter, flies waking up for the summer, but yummy-yummy— *flies!*

Within ten minutes Spid was so full of flies he could hardly move, but still he went on eating. It was hard to stop when there were so many of them and they were so succulent.

Finally he crept back to the guitar case and lay there, gently hiccuping, till he went to sleep.

He was awakened by Norman's voice.

'Why Spid! You are *filthy*! What have you been doing to yourself?'

It had not occurred to Spid that his fly-hunting in the darkest parts of the disco hall might spoil his bright colours and scratch his paint. Each of his eight legs was more tarnished than the last. He had lost his sparkle. The web that had been so splendidly decorated was now broken in three places. He had intended to mend it before the boys came back, but instead, he had fallen asleep. Shame made him appear more dingy still. He half closed his eyes and looked resentfully at Norman.

'Spid! Are you ill?' Norman cried in alarm.

The other boys clustered around.

'He does look off-colour,' said the one called David.

'Get a vet,' somebody suggested.

Norman made an angry exclamation.

'His feet are all dirty too! Spid, where have you been? Have you been out of the case, randying around?

How *could* you, Spid? You're our *star!*'

Spid cringed into the back of the case. It was quite true that in his hunting fervour he had forgotten for the moment how important he was.

'I was hungry,' he muttered. '*Hic!*'

'Well, why didn't you say so?' cried Norman in despair. 'We'd have brought you a hamburger! And now all the kids are arriving and it's too late!'

'I don't want a hamburger,' Spid murmured. '*Hic!*'

'He's got the hiccups,' some of the boys said, greatly amused. 'Come on! Let's get going! He'll soon dance it off!'

But Spid was suffering from such painful indigestion that for a long time he could not even leave his case.

The Grand Opening that Norman had planned, with Spid slowly descending his thread in a blaze of coloured lights in the centre of the stage had to be postponed until he felt well enough to creep out, by which time nearly all the rest of his luminous paint had been rubbed off in his writhings and groanings.

'Come on, Spid!' Norman said impatiently. 'It's time you got on with it. The kids want to know if there really is a spider. Put a match to it!'

Spid staggered out, his stomach aching and rumbling.

He climbed up the wall and across the ceiling to the centre of the stage, where he let himself down on a long, worn thread. The coloured lights picked him out, and the young people on the floor of the hall shouted and waved, but the glory of the spectacle fell flat. The thread was no longer bright with fluorescent paint. The spider did not glitter and sparkle.

To the audience it was still quite a feature. All the lights were focused on the swinging body and its eight waving legs. The rest of the hall was in perfect darkness.

But to Norman and the rest of the group, who knew what the full effect should have been, it was an anticlimax, and they began to play their opening number in a spirit of sulky indignation.

At least, they thought, Spid would now come to life and display his remarkable antics, so that the veiled jeering and a few scornful remarks among the audience would be quenched, and then they would see what the Spider group could do.

But Spid did not come to life. He hung there from his threads like a dead weight on a disused bellpull. Now and again his frame was shaken by a giant hiccup, and his eight legs trembled. He was so afraid of being sick that he dared not dance or even wriggle. He simply closed his eyes and hung there waiting, until after a long, long time the music stopped.

The lights were switched off, and the hall electricity came on again. Norman stretched up, broke the thread, and stuffed Spid into the guitar case, closing the lid.

'I guess we're back again to the Satellites,' he told the group.

## 15

# The Sponsored Spin

On Monday morning Norman met Henry in the playground and thrust an envelope into his hands.

'Here's your rotten spider,' he said fiercely. 'I never want to see it again! It let down my group, and now we are the laughing stock of the district. Don't you let my sister Linda see it, because she'll have it off you if you do. And if it comes back to our place I swear I'll squash it!'

'Thank you,' stammered Henry in astonishment.

He had never expected to see Spid again. When Grandpa's loud cries had been heard at last in the park, he had been rescued by the park keeper, and had related an angry story about going into the park with Spid and being deserted by him when a little girl with curly hair came along and enticed him away.

'*Left* me,' Grandpa kept repeating. 'Left me flat! No feelings! No manners! No consideration! The great, hairy brute!'

Henry now felt at liberty to display Spid at school, where he soon became almost famous. Norman was no longer a threat and even Linda knew that her brother meant what he said. If Spid came into the house again he intended to squash him, and very reluctantly she gave up the idea of having him for a pet.

Everyone had become very animal minded, since the Headmaster announced that it was Animal Week, and

114

special efforts were to be made to support the Royal Society for the Prevention of Cruelty to Animals.

'I think that is a first-rate idea,'Spid said approvingly. 'And the first rule to announce is that I'm not a pet. I'm a spider in my own right!'

'There doesn't seem much point in announcing that,' Henry said, rather provoked by Spid's attitude. 'After all, nobody's hurting you by calling you a pet.'

'It's my feelings is hurt!' returned Spid. 'They all think I'm just a simple spider, but I'll show them I'm not! I'll spin the biggest spider's web in all the world, and then they'll know the kind of person I really am.'

And so the idea of the Giant Sponsored Spider's Web was born.

Henry and his friends asked all their friends and relations to sponsor the number of circles Spid could spin in twelve hours of daylight.

Norman pretended not to be interested, but he hung about the playground watching Spid's activities until Henry asked him to keep a list of the sponsors, after which he became really enthusiastic, and rushed round the school and the neighbourhood, badgering and bullying people for their sponsorships, and persuading them to give more than they intended to afford.

His sister Linda, who had spent all her pocket-money, was in the depths of distress until her mother rescued her, and promised to pay 3p a circle in Linda's name, when the web was completed.

Henry's mother promised the same, and his father

promised 5p. Aunty Bloss offered 2p, and Grandpa flatly refused to pay anything at all.

'Throwing away your money on that miserable spider!' he said contemptuously. 'It will start off like a race track and leave off in the middle. You see if I'm not right!'

Spid glowered at him from the edge of Henry's pocket.

'Then you wouldn't have to pay so much, Grandpa,' Henry encouraged him.

'I wouldn't pay a penny,' Grandpa announced. 'But I'll tell you what I *will* do. If the little rascal actually builds a web that we can all *see*—well, I'll think again!'

Not even Norman could persuade him to make a better offer, and Henry had to be content with that.

The final spot was chosen. The web was to hang in the playground, on the wall of the gymnasium, facing west, so that it would not be too hot for Spid to spin during the heat of the day.

Excitement was rising as at last the day was fixed. Even the Headmaster was taking a keen interest, and the school secretary had made a poster to hang on the wall next to the cobweb. It announced:  'A Sponsored Giant Spider's Web will be spun on Friday, 18th June, in aid of the Royal Society for the Prevention of Cruelty to Animals. The spinning will take place between the hours of 8 a.m. and 8 p.m. All sponsorships must be in by 7.30 p.m. on the previous evening.'

Meanwhile Henry was putting Spid into training.

He had him racing up and down drainpipes, waste-pipes, even chimneys, and rigorously dieting his intake of flies.

'Remember the disco!' he warned him. 'You don't want to let everybody down, do you, especially the animals. If you finish the web there will be all that money coming in to the Fund, and you will be the most famous spider in England!'

'Oh, I'll finish it all right,' said Spid peevishly, 'just as long as nobody interferes with me. No coloured lights and things! I don't mind a little music . . . .'

Norman and his Satellites were persuaded to come and play for Spid during the hours when they were not in school. They were a little reluctant till they found that Spid was in earnest and that the sponsored web had actually been his own idea.

Henry put Spid to bed early on the night before the Spin, after a last series of press-ups on the bedroom floor.

The day promised to be fine. Most people aimed to be in the playground by 8 a.m. to start him off. A few of the dads were there, on their way to work. Most of the mothers were absent, since it was their busy hour, but they had promised to look in during the day, and to be there for the finish.

'If there is a proper finish,' Henry said anxiously, 'because twelve hours is a terribly long time to go on spinning.'

'He can rest,' said Norman. 'He hasn't got to spin

without stopping all day long.'

'I know,' Henry agreed. 'Only if he doesn't make enough circles the money won't come in, and he does mean to make a lot of circles—'

'I shall too!' Spid said, flexing his eight legs, one after another.

The morning broke fine and free. There was hardly a breath of wind, while a faint mist promised sunshine later.

It was a cobweb morning, which Henry took for a good omen. Thousands of tiny spiders had painted their innocent webs across the grass, in a vast counterpane of glistening silver.

Henry trod lightly across the grass. He did not like the idea of crushing all those little Spids, but Spid himself was quite indifferent. Where once he had tried to sweep them away, now he took no notice whatever, but peered ahead, clinging to the flap of Henry's pocket, his eyes on the gate of the playground, his thoughts on the height of the wall he was going to cover.

Other children were hurrying up the road. Quite a large crowd gathered round the gymnasium wall, waiting for the Headmaster to arrive and start off the contest. He came, on a motor-bicycle, just five minutes before eight o'clock.

As the school clock struck eight, Spid climbed out of Henry's pocket and raced to the wall. Up, up he climbed, his eight legs flashing, his furry feet clutching at the roughness of the bricks and forcing him on.

Halfway up the wall he stopped, turned to face the crowd, and waved one or two legs in salutation.

Then he began to spin.

The first circles were so small that five or six were formed very quickly. Round and round went Spid, and by the time school started the Giant Cobweb was well and truly under way. He did not notice the 'good-lucks!' and warm greetings thrown to him over their shoulders as the children trooped into school. The dads had long since departed, and would not be seen again until evening.

It was hard for anyone to concentrate in school until the Headmaster, touring the classrooms, announced that anyone doing a good piece of work would be allowed out of class five minutes early. After that some splendid exercises were sent in, and only a few children remained, sniffing, until the playtime bell.

Spid had not wasted his time. The web, though still small, was visible halfway across the yard. But the children's attention was diverted from Spid by a hooting and shouting from the lane outside the school grounds, where several tradesmen's vans were gathered in a bunch. They were prevented from entering the school drive by a thick rope, quite obviously spun by Spid, on which dangled a page torn from an exercise book.

Across the page was scrawled in scrambly capitals: SPOSRSHP IN PROGRESS.

## NO ENTRY ON BIZNES
## KEEP OUT.

The drivers were rattling and banging at the gate, which was tied up with webs as tough and as strong as wire. When they saw the children they made an even louder noise, and everybody ran over to see what they were shouting about.

'We can't get in! Fetch the boss!' the men shouted.

'It's our dinner they've got there,' said Norman accusingly. 'And it's your rotten spider again, Henry! Why can't he mind his own business?'

'I *am* minding my own business,' said Spid, joining them at the gate. 'It's them that didn't! They came snooping over the yard and disturbing my work and . . . .'

'Hi!' said Norman, seizing the occasion to enlist some more sponsors. He turned to the tradesmen and began to bargain with them. Two children fetched wheelbarrows. The goods were loaded on to the barrows and rushed to the kitchens, while the drivers, tiptoeing as close as they dared to Spid's cobweb, watched him take up the thread where he had left off, and readily promised to add their money to the rest if he had really covered the wall by the end of the day.

'We'll let the Press know,' they promised, driving away, 'and we'll be back for the finish.'

'There!' Henry encouraged Spid. 'You'll be in the newspapers now, and you'll like that, won't you?'

'Yes,' said Spid, 'but I'm getting rather tired

of spinning.'

'Oh Spid!' all the children moaned. 'You've only just begun! Are you hungry? Are you thirsty? Would you like a fly?'

'One dead fly, and one tiny drink of water,' Henry commanded. 'Go on Spid! You know you can spin for hours! Think of the animals!'

'I don't like animals,' retorted Spid. He dropped to the ground and lay there motionless, looking like a twisted-up elastic band.

The situation was saved by Norman's Satellite group, who came racing over from the bicycle shed and began to play at full strength. In no time Spid was up the wall again and jiggling and jogging to the tune.

Everybody cheered, and fifteen circles could be counted on the web, each one bigger than the last, and joined to its neighbour by a ladder of little silver bars.

'It's *beautiful,*' said all the little girls.

'That's right,' Spid agreed cheerfully.

'Go it, feller! You're great!' shouted the boys, above the playing of the Satellites.

The bell shrilled for the end of playtime.

'Now don't you give up while we are gone,' Henry told Spid. 'We'll be back at dinner-time . . . more music . . . another fly . . . .'

'*Two* flies!' said Spid.

'All right—two *little* flies—only don't stop spinning, will you? Promise?'

'It's hard work,' grumbled Spid.

121

Dinner hour came. An hour's break, and this time the whole school turned out to admire the Giant Cobweb which was beginning at last to be worthy of its name. Quite half of the wall was covered with silver threads, and twenty circles, now becoming enormous, crept outwards from the centre, where for the moment Spid was taking a nap. He came to life when the admiring audience arrived, and began to scuttle round the outside of his web, spinning madly, as if he had never left off.

'Poor little mite,' said one of the kitchen staff. 'It seems a shame to expect all that much from one little creature!'

Spid was so grateful to her he dropped off the wall and ran to kiss her feet, causing chaos, as the whole of the kitchen staff ran back to the kitchen screaming.

'Oh Spid! You should have had more sense!' Henry scolded, as he picked up the spider and put him back on the web. Spid sulked for a moment, and then set to work again, spurred on by the crowd's admiration and the tuning-up of the Satellites, who were prepared to play all through their lunch hour, taking it in turns to go to dinner.

By the end of the lunch hour Spid had developed new courage and determination. His sulkiness was gone, his legs fairly galloped round the great web. All the morning's apathy had vanished. He hardly seemed to notice the Satellites, nor turn his head when the bell rang and they had to stop playing and go in to school.

His jiggling had stopped a long time ago. It was as if he needed every ounce of strength for his spinning, and he did not even pause to talk to Henry.

By half past three the web was enormous.

Spid was working more slowly now, climbing round the outside and dragging his long, silver thread behind him. One after another the knots were tied and the little bars were fixed. The outer circle slowly grew. There were fifty circles now, and although each one took longer and longer to spin, the whole web was a formidable display of craftsmanship and creative art.

The Headmaster said as much when school was over. He came out to inspect Spid's masterpiece.

'A real piece of creative art,' he pronounced. 'You want to take it easy now, old man!' he said to Spid. 'We'll all come back and look at it at eight o'clock, and pay our dues. I've told the Press, and the Mayor is coming, and I've no doubt there will be some television coverage. I don't know how many circles you have made, but there must be well over fifty.'

'I am going to make a hundred!' said Spid grimly, toiling away. 'No more music, thank you, I can only give my attention to one thing at a time. I have got to the stage where I must be left alone to work in peace.'

'Well done! Well done!' said the Headmaster. 'Goodbye, old chap! We'll see you later!'

'Goodbye sir,' said Spid politely. He waved an aching leg and went on spinning.

Reluctantly, Henry went home to tea.

Clouds gathered, and the sun went out of the sky. Spid was quite relieved, for the afternoon had been very hot.

Now all his attention was on the Great Web. He was almost awed by his own effort. Never in his life, nor in the lives of his ancestors, had he imagined seeing such a beautiful cobweb. He hoped that the Headmaster would cover it with a sheet of glass when it was finished, and keep it on the wall of the gymnasium for ever, with his name: 'SPID' underneath it.

But it had got to be a hundred circles wide, for the sake of history and *The Guinness Book of Records,* from which Henry was always quoting.

'The biggest spider web ever spun . . . ' Spid murmured to himself, 'was a hundred circles wide, spun by a spider called Spid in the year 1985, and sponsored by over two hundred people. It was spun in aid of the Royal Society for the Prevention of Cruelty to Animals, and raised the magnificent sum of . . . .' Spid could not work out how much money the web would raise if he achieved his hundred circles.

A low rumble of thunder made him jump. Spid hated thunderstorms. They reverberated down the drains and washed spiders down strange wastepipes.

Time was racing on—it was nearly seven o'clock, and what would become of the Giant Web if he left it to the mercy of the thunderstorm?

A spiteful little wind came gusting across the playground and whistled round the corner of the school, raising the cobweb like a sheet on a clothes-line, and slapping it back against the wall.

Spid gave a shriek and flew to tether the loose ends. Another gust like that and his precious work would be ruined. Feverishly he tied down the ends and mended two or three of the strands that had parted.

Another gust of wind arrived, and another portion of the web was raised up, tugging at the wall as if it wanted to free itself and fly away, like some great, enormous flying carpet.

Spid raced across the middle of the web and tied it down, while suddenly the heavens opened, and down came the rain in a solid sheet.

Spid was almost grateful to see it. He knew his web would support quite a lot of water, and now that the rain was falling there was not so much wind.

And within minutes the playground was full of children, led by Henry—children with umbrellas, children with groundsheets, children with macintoshes. They surrounded Spid with a wall of defence against the storm, except that the rain was falling straight down from the sky and there was no way of covering the gymnasium wall.

But the Giant Web held fast against the rain, every bar and cross-thread sparkling with silver drops. It was an even more beautiful sight than before the thunderstorm, and round it the children clustered, splashing with their gumboots in the puddles, encouraging and praising Spid, who worked feverishly to finish the last few circles before time ran out.

The grown-ups began to arrive, chasing their children, but the storm was moving away now. As the black clouds vanished the sun came out again.

Henry's parents arrived, and Mrs Gridley, and Aunty Bloss, and, most unexpectedly, Grandpa in a taxi. Henry rushed to find him a chair, and sat him down quite close to Spid, where he could see what was going on.

'Ninety-seven . . . ninety-eight . . . ' said Grandpa, looking at his watch. 'He'll never do it!'

Spid was very tired.

The clock on the school gable announced ten minutes to eight, and the last circle was hardly begun. The Satellites were playing madly to encourage him. The whole school was yelling his name. Henry, close to Spid's side, was shouting encouragement and trembling with excitement as he urged him on.

'Is the Press here?' panted Spid.

'Yes—oh yes!' said Henry, one eye on the reporters writing in little notebooks.

'And the television?' whispered Spid.

'Yes . . . no . . . yes . . . I don't think so! Oh yes, here they are!' cried Henry in great relief as the television van rattled in through the gate.

Spid made a final effort, and spun the last six inches of the Giant Web just before the clock struck eight.

The children went on cheering for quite five minutes.

Meanwhile the Press were questioning Henry, and

the television people took a sequence that they had nearly missed through being late. Spid took quite a lot of persuading to climb the wall again and pretend to be spinning some more thread.

'But don't you *want* to be seen on television?' Henry urged him.

Spid did, and presently the Press and the television people went away, and Norman began to collect the money from the various sponsors.

When he came to Grandpa the old man put his hand in his pocket and brought out a five pound note.

'That's my spider!' Grandpa said. 'I knew he'd do it!'

Norman regretted giving Spid back to Henry, but the Satellite group had been noticed by the Press, and all their names taken for the papers. After all, you couldn't have everything.

The hero of the day was asleep, utterly exhausted, in Henry's pocket, having earned £350 for the Royal Society for the Prevention of Cruelty to Animals.

'I'll sign autographs in the morning,' he told Henry.

# 16

## Till Death Us Do Part

In the morning Spid was still asleep when the news-papers came. There was quite a lot about him on the front page.

'Henry's spinner is a winner!' the headlines said, but then they went on to describe Spid as 'Henry's pet spider', and Henry knew that Spid would not care about that.

Spid slept all day, and only woke up for the six o'clock news.

'Is there anything about me?' he asked, crawling on to Henry's knee.

There was. There was a scene from the school playground, with all the children and their parents and the tradesmen and the Headmaster, all watching Spid spinning the Giant Web.

'Young Henry had a bright idea,' said the announcer. 'He founded a sponsorship for his pet spider, who, under Henry's direction, spun a Giant Cobweb on the walls of the school, sponsored by about two hundred of Henry's friends. The splendid sum of £350 was made by Henry for the Royal Society for the Prevention of Cruelty to Animals.'

'Isn't that lovely?' said Aunty Bloss, who was spending the evening with the Pratts.

Spid did his elastic band act. He lay on Henry's knees with every leg twisted underneath him, looking

129

as dead as an autumn leaf, and not nearly so attractive.

'It's ever so good of Henry,' said Aunty Bloss, taking no notice of him.

Presently Henry carried Spid, still crumpled up, to his bedroom and gave him some supper. Spid refused either to eat or to speak to him.

'It isn't my fault,' said Henry bitterly, 'I *told* them it was your idea, and that you were my *friend* . . . I can't help it if they get it all wrong!'

'What did the newspapers say?' Spid asked, opening one eye.

'Much the same.'

'Oh.'

'Oh Spid, don't be so *silly*!' Henry cried. 'You're famous, can't you see it? You've woven the biggest cobweb in the world! It has been photographed for television! Aren't you PROUD?'

'Do they want me to sign autographs?' Spid asked hopefully.

Nobody had thought about it. It had not occurred to anybody that Spid could write. They thought the KEEP OUT notice board had been written by Henry.

'I'll tell them all on Monday,' Henry promised, but Spid was not interested.

'It's too late,' he said crossly. 'All that work for nothing! All day long . . . so hot! . . . All my legs aching! And even Grandpa didn't believe in me!'

'He gave five pounds to the Fund,' Henry reminded him. 'And just look how much money you made for the animals!'

'It's *not* for the animals,' Spid snapped. 'It's to stop people being cruel to them, and if they've got to be cruel to me to stop people being cruel to the animals then I don't think it was a good idea after all. And I'm *not* your pet, Henry—I'm Spid, I'm the Star Spider, the Record Giant Web Spinner. I'm ME!'

'I know, Spid. I'm sorry Spid,' said Henry humbly.

'So I'm going to leave you, Henry!' Spid went on as if Henry had not spoken. 'I can see I'll never be understood here, however hard I try. Besides, I want to get married.'

'You *what!*' exclaimed Henry, who could not believe his ears.

'Well, what's wrong with that?' asked Spid crossly. 'Everybody gets married at some time or another. Grandpa did, your parents did, Mrs Gridley did! Aunty Bloss didn't but that's her affair. You will get married yourself sooner or later!'

'Much later,' said Henry, horrified. 'But have you . . . have you got a *bride*?'

'No, of course not,' snapped Spid. 'How could I have, with the life I've been leading here? I've got to find one. And that's another thing. I simply haven't got time to sign any autographs . . . .'

'But *where* will you find a wife?' asked Henry.

'I thought you would help me,' Spid said, with a more agreeable note in his voice. 'After all, you can take me to places, museums, and places like that.'

'Museums!' exclaimed Henry, very pleased to know he was not to lose Spid immediately. 'Do you want *that* kind of a wife, then? An in . . . in . . . tell . . . ect . . . u-al?'

'No, I don't,' said Spid. 'All right then! Take me down to Grandpa's and we'll hunt in his sheds.'

But when they arrived at Grandpa's the old gentleman wanted Spid to come back and live with him and to help him in and out of his chair.

'You wouldn't let an old friend down, would you, Spider boy?' Grandpa wheedled.

'No, I wouldn't,' Spid agreed. 'Only, you see, I'm going to be married!'

'Married?' cried Grandpa. He was just as shocked as Henry. 'Who are you getting married to, I'd like to know?'

'Spid is looking for a wife,' Henry explained. 'We thought we might possibly find one in your sheds, Grandpa.'

'Help yourselves!' said Grandpa in a huff. 'As far as I am aware I don't keep any spider's wives in my outhouses. But by all means make certain.'

Grandpa was quite right. There were no spiders in the sheds, and although they found a few in various other places Spid was so rude about them that in the end Henry asked him:

'Are you sure you really want to get married?'

'Yes, of course I do,' said Spid. 'But I'm not going to marry just anybody. . . . '

During the night the wind had come back and torn the giant web off the gymnasium wall. It hung in tatters, too ruined to photograph. 'And all that work I did!' said Spid. He seemed to blame Henry for the damage.

In desperation Henry appealed to Norman, and the next day the Satellites brought quite a big collection of spiders of all shapes and sizes to parade in front of Spid, who received them very coolly.

'That one's a boy. . . . That one's ugly! So's that one! That's a *he* too . . . couldn't you tell? And that old thing is a grandma! That one's not much better! Aren't there *any* pretty spiders about? Can't you find something that is worth looking at? Would *you* want to marry a miserable little creature like that one? Aren't I worth something much better than the kind of rubbish you have got here? Remember, I'm Super Spid. I'm ME!'

Henry became quite exasperated with him, and the Satellites would have lost interest if they had not been so impressed by Spid's performance of the day before.

Finally Henry took him home, and hoped he would forget about getting married.

'You could settle down and live so happily with the rest of us,' he said.

'You don't understand me,' said Spid. 'I want to be friends, but I want to be understood as well. I don't want to be anybody's pet, but everybody wants to own me and to make me do things. I believe only a wife can really understand me and make me happy.'

133

'Oh I *do* understand you, Spid, and I love you,' said Henry. 'And people want you for a pet because they love you too. It's a nice name to be called.'

'You didn't like being called Teacher's Pet,' said Spid nastily. 'You hit Norman on the nose for it! Well, I can't hit the television crew and Aunty Bloss and Grandpa and the Headmaster, but I'm not going near them any more! I've finished with the lot of you! And if I can't be married I'm going back home where I belong. Goodbye Henry! You're a nice boy, and I have enjoyed being friends with you, but it is all over now. Give my love to Norman and Linda! And the Satellites! Goodbye! Goodbye!'

As Spid talked he was hurrying across the floor in the direction of the bathroom. Henry could not catch up with him. He arrived in the doorway just in time to see the spider climbing up the side of the bath and dropping down the inside of it. The next moment he had scuttled into the wastepipe, stopping only long enough to wave first one long leg and then another.

Henry stood in the doorway, perfectly transfixed with grief and shock.

'Oh do come back, Spid,' he pleaded.

'Goodbye! Goodbye!' called Spid, his voice becoming fainter and fainter as he climbed down the pipe.

'Spid!' Henry protested, leaning over the bath. 'Don't go away, Spid! It's going to be awful without you!'

No answer came back from the wastepipe. Henry

listened in vain. For nearly half an hour he waited and called and listened. His mother found him in tears, and she listened too.

Finally his father came into the bathroom, and shouted down the plughole:

'Spid! Come back, old man! We need you! Come on, Spid! Don't lurk there sulking! We're all waiting for you up here!'

Henry ran to summon the Satellites, who brought their music and played frenziedly for twenty minutes. There was not the faintest response from the bathpipe.

Everybody went away except Henry.

He had his supper beside the bath, and stayed there waiting and listening until he went to bed.

Nobody enjoyed their baths in the morning. If felt so final to jam down the plug into the plughole and to turn on the taps. But it made no difference at all. There was not the faintest sign of Spid.

He had said his goodbyes and vanished for good.

Henry searched for him in all his old haunts, up and down the streets, calling down the drains, even in the park.

Nobody had seen him, not Grandpa, not Aunty Bloss, not Mrs Gridley.

'I told you so!' said Grandpa. 'Leaves a job half done, just as I said he would! But anyway, I don't need him to help me now, I can get up by myself!'

Linda would have been heartbroken, only she had discovered a large and furry caterpillar, and was allow-ing it to make itself a cocoon in the best bedroom of her dolls' house.

It was Henry who grieved the most, and even he was prepared never to see Spid again.

Then, one afternoon, as he loitered out of habit in the bathroom, he heard the faintest scratching noise down the wastepipe.

Henry rushed to remove the plug, and slung it round the cold tap.

The noise stopped.

Then it began again, and Henry sat trembling with expectation on the edge of the bath, not daring to speak or move.

It was a long, long way up the wastepipe, but the scratching noise went on and on, as if the climber inside it were still climbing.

As Henry watched, first one leg came out and then another, and then another, and then another, and then another, and then another, and then another, and then another.

Spid had arrived.

Henry was about to rush at him and take him into his arms when the spider held up a warning leg. He turned back towards the plughole.

'Come along, my pet,' Spid cooed.

Out of the plughole came a long golden silky leg, followed by seven more. When all the legs were out they were followed by the most beautiful golden body, and Henry saw before him the prettiest spider he had ever seen or imagined in the whole of his life.

'My wife!' Spid said proudly. 'Not come to stay, you realise! Just to visit. Henry, I have discovered her at last! This is my wife! And this, my pet, is Henry!'

*Other great reads* ⭐ *from* **Red Fox**

## Red Fox Animal Stories

**FOWL PEST**
(Shortlisted for the Smarties Prize)
James Andrew Hall
Amy Pickett wants to be a chicken! Seriously! Understandably her family aren't too keen on the idea. Even Amy's best friend, Clarice, thinks she's unhinged. Then Madam Marvel comes to town and strange feathery things begin to happen.
*A Fantastic tale, full of jokes*
**Child Education**
0 09 940182 7   £2.99

**OMELETTE: A CHICKEN IN PERIL**
Gareth Owen
As the egg breaks, a young chicken pops his head out of the crack to see, with horror, an enormous frying pan. And so Omelette is born into the world! This is just the beginning of a hazardous life for the wide-eyed chicken who must learn to keep his wits about him.
0 09 940013 8   £2.99

**ESCAPE TO THE WILD**
Colin Dann
Eric made up his mind. He would go to the pet shop, open the cages and let the little troupe of animals escape to the wild.
*Readers will find the book unputdownable*
**Growing Point**
0 09 940063 4   £2.99

**SEAL SECRET**
Aidan Chambers
William is really fed up on holliday in Wales until Gwyn, the boy from the nearby farm, shows him the seal lying in a cave. Gwyn knows exactly what he is going to do with it; William knows he has to stop him . . .
0 09 99150 0   £2.99

## Part **1** of the City Cats Series

Colin Dann

# King of the Vagabonds

*By the creator of the award-winning*
*THE ANIMALS OF FARTHING WOOD*

*Incredible animal adventures starring*
*furry felines, Sammy and Pinkie...*

'Don't stray into Quartermile Field. Any animal with sense avoids the spot,' warns Sammy's mother. But Sammy is curious - about the Field, and about his father, the fierce, wild father he's never met.

Then one day Sammy discovers that his father has returned. And determined to track him down, Sammy sets off towards the strange, wild land of Quartermile Field - and into a very different and dangerous world...

THE CITY CATS SERIES by Colin Dann
in paperback from Red Fox

KING OF THE VAGABONDS
ISBN 0 09 921192 0    £3.50

THE CITY CATS
ISBN 0 09 921202 1    £3.50

COPYCAT
ISBN 0 09 21212 9    £3.99

Part **2** of the City Cats Series

## Colin Dann

# The City Cats

*By the creator of the award-winning*
*THE ANIMALS OF FARTHING WOOD*

*Incredible animal adventures starring*
*furry felines, Sammy and Pinkie...*

Scavenging for food in the back of a van leads Sammy
and Pinkie into trouble when they suddenly find
themselves trapped - and travelling. They arrive in a
scary place, full of fast cars and strange people, but a
park provides shelter and a fat pigeon makes a fine meal.
Sammy's still the proud King of the Vagabonds and
Pinkie's looking forward to having a family. As big city
cats they've finally found the good life. But how long can
it last...?

THE CITY CATS SERIES by Colin Dann
in paperback from Red Fox

KING OF THE VAGABONDS
ISBN 0 09 921192 0    £3.50

THE CITY CATS
ISBN 0 09 921202 1    £3.50

COPYCAT
ISBN 0 09 21212 9    £3.99

*Other great reads* from **Red Fox**

Whatever you like to read, Red Fox has got the story for you. Why not choose another book from our range of Animal Stories, Funny Stories or Fantastic Stories? Reading has never been so much fun!

## Red Fox Funny Stories

### THANKS FOR THE SARDINE
Laura Beaumont

Poor Aggie is sick and tired of hearing her mates jabbering on about how brilliant their Aunties are. Aggie's aunties are useless. In fact they're not just boring – they don't even try! Could a spell at Aunt Augusta's Academy of Advanced Auntiness be the answer?

*Chucklesome stuff!*
**Young Telegraph**

### GIZZMO LEWIS: FAIRLY SECRET AGENT
Michael Coleman

Gizzmo Lewis, newly qualified secret agent from the planet Sigma-6, is on a mission. He's been sent to check out the defences of a nasty little planet full of ugly creatures – yep, you guessed it, he's on planet Earth! It's all a shock to Gizzmo's system so he decides to sort things out – alien-style!
0 09 926631 8   £2.99

### THE HOUSE THAT SAILED AWAY
Pat Hutchins
It has rained all holiday! But just as everyone is getting really fed up of being stuck indoors, the house starts to shudder and rock, and then just floats off down the street to the sea. Hungry cannibals, bloody-thirsty pirates and a cunning kidnapping are just some of the hair-raisers in store.
0 09 993200 8   £2.99

# ❖ Tales of Redwall ❖
# BRIAN JACQUES

'Not since Roald Dahl have children filled their
shelves so compulsively' *The Times*

*An award-winning, best-selling series from
master storyteller, Brian Jacques.
Discover the epic* Tales of Redwall *adventures
about Redwall Abbey - and beyond!*

- **Martin the Warrior**   0 09 928171 6
- **Mossflower**   0 09 955400 3
- **Outcast of Redwall**   0 09 960091 9
- **Mariel of Redwall**   0 09 992960 0
- **The Bellmaker**   0 09 943331 1
- **Salamandastron**   0 09 914361 5
- **Redwall**   0 09 951200 9
- **Mattimeo**   0 09 967540 4
- **The Pearls of Lutra**   0 09 963871 1

Tales of Redwall by Brian Jacques
Out now in paperback from Red Fox priced £4.99

RANDOM HOUSE
LIBRARY